# YELLOW BIRD AND ME

## JOYCE HANSEN

**CLARION BOOKS**

NEW YORK

For my students
and for the
Nataki Talibah Schoolhouse

Clarion Books
a Houghton Mifflin Company imprint
215 Park Avenue South, New York, NY 10003
Copyright © 1986 by Joyce Hansen
All rights reserved.
For information about permission to reproduce
selections from this book write to Permissions,
Houghton Mifflin Company, 215 Park Avenue South, New York, NY 10003.
Printed in the USA

Library of Congress Cataloging in Publication Data. Hansen, Joyce. Yellow Bird
and me. Sequel to: The gift-giver. Summary: Doris becomes friends with Yellow
Bird as she helps him with his studies and his part in the school play and dis-
covers that he has a problem known as dyslexia.   1. Children's stories, Ameri-
can.   [1. Friendship—Fiction.   2. Dyslexia—Fiction.   3. Schools—Fiction]
I. Title. PZ7.H19825Ye   1986      [Fic]      85—484      ISBN 0-89919-335-8
PA ISBN 0-395-55388-1
QUM 20   19   18   17   16

# CONTENTS ƧTИƎTИO०

October 20th

My Dear Amir,

163rd Street is dingy gray even though the leaves on the trees are gold and red and orange. I bet upstate is much more beautiful. I still feel sad when I think about how you had to go away. It was wrong that your foster family put you in a home and didn't take you with them to California. Anyway, at least Syracuse is closer to the Bronx than California is.

I'm glad you was put into the eighth grade where you belong. What is it like in the group home? Do all of you live in one big building? Like an institution or something? Did you find any of your brothers and sisters yet? Hope you do soon. Did you make any friends or do you stay by yourself like you showed me how to do?

Everything changed since you left. I don't be with Mickey and Dotty, the twins, and Lavinia much anymore. They all stuck up and mean this year.

Big Russell, T.T., and Yellow Bird haven't changed though. They the same — playing basketball and bothering decent people. Russell lost some weight but he's still the biggest kid in the sixth grade. And Yellow Bird with his pale, long-nose self. He still flies around like a little bird. Lately he's been acting silly as ever and bugging me about helping him with his school work.

Are you lonely, Amir? I guess you are. I am too. Seems like I have no one to talk to the way I could talk to you. I'm going to figure out how to come up-state to visit you. It ain't been the same here since you left.

It's imperative (new word we learned from our teacher) that you write soon. I don't have no one else to talk to. Anyway, I don't let things bother me the way I used to. I'm doing real good in school so far and I hope to make the honor roll. I haven't been under punishment for a month.

I'm sending you a poem. Maybe you can draw a picture to go with it. Do you still draw beautiful pictures?

Please, please, please write soon.

> Your friend to the end,
> Love,
> Doris

I read over the letter, then folded it and slipped it inside of my bag. I needed to find a quiet place to write my poem for Amir, so I escaped into the library to get away from the schoolyard, where my friends played and teased and acted as if everything was the same — as if Amir was still around. Even though Amir had been gone from our block for a month, I still missed him as if he'd only left yesterday. Losing a best friend is one of the worst things that can happen to you.

The clock on the wall said 8:15. Twenty minutes before it was time to line up for classes. The librarian allowed no talking above a whisper. The carpet on the floor even smothered the sound of footsteps. Three second graders at the table next to mine quietly read a picture book.

I sat at my usual spot by the window and tried to think up a poem for Amir. I stared out of the window and the building across the street stared back at me. A woman on the third floor opened her window and waved to someone passing in the street below. I wrote the first line:

*A friend is like a crown of rubies,*

"Yo, Doris!" Yellow Bird, whose name is really James Towers, called to me loudly from the library entrance. The librarian frowned at him and put her finger to her lips. He covered his mouth and opened his eyes wide. "I'm sorry," he croaked in a hoarse, loud whisper.

Why did he have to find me when I was in the middle of writing an important poem?

He burst through the doorway and made his way over to my table. His jacket hung off his shoulders and his elbows stuck straight out like wings. I covered the line I'd written with my hand. "What you want, Bird?" I whispered.

"Nothing. Just come here to study."

I didn't believe him. Bird never studied unless he had too. "The only thing you study is a basketball," I said.

He spread his books and papers all over the table. He looked worried and more birdlike than ever. "My father said he's taking me off the basketball team if I bring home another bad report card."

"So you want help?"

"I didn't ask for help. I already did all of my homework. Just have to finish reading these last four pages. I don't need no help."

Before he came I'd had peace and quiet. I also had a nice, empty neat table all to myself. I tried to get back to my poem, but was distracted when he opened his social studies book and noisily rustled through the pages.

I picked up my things and started to move to another table. "Doris, stay here. I ain't gonna bother you. Promise. Just make believe I ain't here." He rustled some more papers.

"That's impossible," I said, standing up to move.

He batted his eyelashes. "Doris, please stay." He leaned into me and grinned.

"Bird, I'll pop you upside your head if you don't get out of my face." I put my papers back down on the table and tried to work again as he concentrated on his book, turning the pages quickly and noisily. I stared at the one line I'd written before he found me, and then out the window. As a large, puffy white cloud rolled across the sky, I wrote the next line:

*beautiful and rare.*

Bird tapped me on the shoulder. "What's this word?"

"*Pharaoh,*" I snapped. "You said you wasn't gonna bug me."

"I know the rest." He cleared his throat, crossed his legs, and reared back in his chair.

I studied what I'd written so far. I could just see Amir now, reading my poem. He'd be so happy to hear from me. I knew he was lonelier than me in that home upstate, and my letter and poem would really cheer him up. I thought of the next line for my poem:

*You're the most precious jewel of all . . .*

Bird nudged me with his elbow. "Doris, what's this word here?" he whispered loudly.

"I thought you knew the rest."

"I do. I just don't know this word." His index finger dug into the page.

"Country," I said, turning back to my poem.

He put his head back in the book and then I felt another tap on my shoulder. I thought I was going to strangle Bird.

"Remember how you and Amir used to write down important dates for me to memorize when we studied for the social studies tests?"

"Of course I remember," I said.

"Why can't you help me now, like you and him used to when we was in the fifth grade together?"

"Because things are different now."

"How?" He frowned, and pouted like a little kid.

"Amir was the one who helped you, and he ain't here."

"You could do the same thing he did." He popped out of his seat and held my shoulders. "Doris, please. You're the only one who can save the basketball team."

I pushed him away. "Sometimes you talk crazy. What does the basketball team have to do with it?"

"If my father takes me off the team, they'll lose. I'm the star player. Help me, Doris. Do it for the team. For Dunbar Elementary School."

The librarian looked at us again. "If you two continue to make noise, you'll have to leave."

I threw a crumpled piece of paper at him. "See, you always make someone get in trouble."

"The team is in trouble. They need me to confuse our opponents."

I sucked my teeth. "You don't really want to study, Bird. You only want me to do your homework. You play around too much."

"I'm not playing around. I want to do better." He made a gloomy, sad face. "I want to do good this year, but the work is harder now. I can't do it. I'm afraid I'm not going to pass the sixth grade if I don't start doing better."

He lowered his head. "Doris, do you have time to help me until the bell rings? Please?"

I wouldn't be able to write the poem as long as he was around. I put it in my bag. "Just till the bell rings. And this ain't gonna be no everyday thing."

"We only have ten minutes. You read the last two pages to me, and I'll remember it better."

"You want me to do all the work."

"No. I just want you to read." He shifted uncomfortably in his seat and rubbed his head. It takes too long if I read it by myself."

I read the remaining pages about ancient Egypt while he followed along. The bell rang just as I finished. We raced out of the library, and Bird jumped down the steps, two at a time. Mrs. Barker, our teacher, hates us to be late lining up for class.

Most of the class was already on line in the cafeteria. The first ones on line were Mickey and Dotty, the un-identical twins. The only thing alike about them is that they're both short. Usually they don't dress anything alike; however, today they wore straight yellow skirts and red ribbons tied around a puff of hair on top of their heads. They looked like two lollipops. The twins were so busy gossiping with Lavinia, who was standing behind them, that they didn't see me.

As she talked, Lavinia bounced around with one hand on her hip while waving her other hand back and forth like she was conducting a band.

Lavinia lives on Union Avenue, and we call her *The Daily News* because she tells everyone about everything that happens in the five blocks between Union Avenue, 163rd Street, the playground, and the school.

Lavinia looks older than the rest of us. Her hair is braided with gold and silver beads that end in a perfectly straight row across her shoulders. I wish I had beads like those, I thought.

Towards the end of the line was Big Russell. He carried a basketball under one arm and his books under the other. He frowned when he saw Bird. "Where you been, man? We was looking for you all morning."

T.T., who also lives on Union Avenue, stepped out of line behind Russell and blocked Bird. "I wanted to show you some new moves I been practicing for the game," he said.

Bird surprised Russell and grabbed the basketball out of his hands. "The only move you can show me is to move out of my way," Bird answered, darting back and forth, dribbling the basketball.

"Where was you this morning?" Russell asked again.

"With Doris. She's going to help me study so I can save the team," he shouted for the entire cafeteria to hear.

T.T. snatched the ball from Russell. "I'm the one that's going to save the team," he said.

Before I could say anything, a short, fat shadow crossed the floor. "Class 6-3 QUIET ON THAT LINE!" Most of us stopped talking and clowning around, as we followed Mrs. Barker to our room.

I'd have to let Bird know, I thought, as I walked through the long hallway, that things had changed from the way it used to be when me and Amir helped him study. Amir was gone, and I was sad. I just wanted to be alone to remember how fine it was when the two of us was together. And Yellow Bird was the last person on this earth that I wanted to be bothered with.

Barker stood in front of the room taking attendance, looking like a general in her navy blue suit.

Mickey sat with me and Dotty. Lavinia was on the other side of the room, running her mouth to the boy sitting next to her.

Mickey turned to me. "So, you going to tutor the Bird?"

"No," I answered.

"Why did he say you would?" she asked, looking at me slyly.

"How should I know?" I snapped.

Mrs. Barker clapped her hands. "Doris, no more talking. Class, your attention."

I sat sideways, turning my back to Mickey. The twins and I had classes together since the first grade. Anytime they talked to me, *I* got caught with my mouth open. When classes started in September, I sat in the front of the room to get away from them. The second day of class, Barker rearranged seats, and I ended up in the middle of the first row near Mickey and Dotty again.

Mrs. Barker put her roll book on her desk. "Class, we will now review the social studies homework. Who can tell me when King Tutankhamen reigned?"

Bird's hand shot up in the air before anyone else even opened their books. He sat one row away from me. "I know. . . . I know it," he yelled excitedly.

Mrs. Barker looked annoyed, but she said, "Okay, James." I guess she thought he was going to say something crazy, as usual, to make everyone laugh.

"King Tut reigned in the Eighteenth Dynasty of the New Kingdom," he shouted and then peeped at me. I made believe I didn't see him.

"Thank you, James." Her eyes swept the room. "Is it known how the king died?"

Bird's hand flew in the air again. She nodded toward him.

"No one knows for sure how he died. Maybe he was killed." He'd remembered everything I'd read to him.

Mickey leaned over to me. "What happened to *him*?"

I ignored her and gazed out of the window. Poor Amir, I thought, all by himself in that home. I had to figure out how I was going to save some money so I could go upstate and visit him. I didn't get an allowance. I was too young to work in a restaurant like the high school kids. I could baby-sit, maybe. Except I helped my mother mind my baby brother, Gerald. Maybe I could —

"Doris Williams! Do you know the answer?" Barker interrupted my thoughts.

I hadn't heard a word she'd said. "Oh, ah . . . what was the question again, Mrs. Barker?"

"Young lady, get your mind back here in this room. Now tell me the year his tomb was first discovered."

"Whose tomb?" I asked, my face going blank.

Big Russell let out a loud hoot from the back of the room.

"Doris, you're supposed to be a good student. I'm disappointed."

I hated for Mrs. Barker to do that. Next thing Mickey and them would be talking about Miss Goody-Goody Two Shoes. Someone moaned, and Lavinia sighed real loud.

Bird waved his hands wildly. "I know what it is. I know. . . . I know."

Barker stared at me. "I'm waiting, Doris."

Bird couldn't hold it in. "1922," he blurted.

Barker wheeled around and got red in the face. "You can't behave for more than five minutes, young man. Don't call out." Then she turned to me again. "I expect better than this from you, Doris." She swung her gaze away from me and found another victim. A sleepy-eyed boy who couldn't remember anything about Tut's tomb either.

The next time I looked up, Barker had written out fractions from one end of the board to the other. I hated math, but at least she didn't talk as much for a math lesson as she did when she taught history and English. After she'd finished writing, she asked for a volunteer to solve the first problem.

Lavinia's the math whiz. She strutted up to the blackboard, sucked her lips into her mouth, and cocked her head to the side like she was solving the hardest math problem in the world. Her numbers were large and clear as she quickly worked out the problem.

The light from the window fell on her gold and silver beads. They jingled as she wrote, and sparkled like tiny round pieces of sun and moon. I'd get beads for my braids too, I thought. Except mine would be red and orange and rust, like the fall leaves.

Suddenly the idea came to me. Beads. Hair. Braids. Cornrows. Miss Bee, the hairdresser on 163rd Street. A girl about my age who used to live on the block once worked for her. After school I'd ask Miss Bee if I could work there. If she'd let me, I could pay for a trip to see Amir.

I took the poem out of my bag and placed it between the pages of my notebook. I needed something to rhyme with beautiful and rare. As I watched Russell slowly divide $2\frac{3}{4}$ by $1\frac{1}{4}$ the rest of the poem came to me. I wrote it quickly and read the whole poem.

> A friend is like a crown of rubies,
>    beautiful and rare.
> You're the most precious jewel of all
>    the one, the only Amir.
>
> > With all my love,
> > Doris

"Psst, Doris. What you reading?" Mickey asked, leaning over me and nearly toppling off her seat. I almost choked from her perfume. It was probably her idea to dress like a lollipop.

I quickly closed the book. "Nothing," I said.

"Don't lie. You was reading a letter. A love letter?" She smirked.

Barker stared at me. "Doris Williams, if you're not talking math, then you shouldn't have anything to say."

Mickey and Dotty giggled.

"And why is your notebook closed, Doris?" Barker continued.

Lavinia stared at me from the other side of the room. When I opened the book, my poem fell out. I snatched it off the floor, and Barker saw it.

"What's that?" she asked. "You know you're not to pass around notes. Now give me that."

"But Mrs. Barker, I wasn't passing notes. . . . I —"

"Give. It. To. Me." Barker was death on note passing ever since she found one that Big Russell wrote saying that she looked like a construction worker in a dress. She either destroyed notes or read them aloud.

"I wasn't doing anything," I pleaded.

She stretched her hands out for the poem and moved towards me. I didn't know which was worse — her tearing up the note, or reading it to the class. Bird raised his hand and stood up.

" 'Scuse me, Mrs. Barker, ma'am. That's my note. See, Doris helped me study this morning in the library cause she's smart and all, and anyway, she was helping me read a note someone sent me and see, she put it in her bag then by mistake when the bell rang, and —"

"Sit down and be quiet!" Bird sat down fast like

someone had pushed him back in his seat. I wish he'd mind his own business.

"The brave Bird tries to save Doris," T.T. called out.

"But he cannot help her," Russell finished.

Barker slammed her ruler on her desk, and everyone got quiet. I decided I'd tear the poem up if she tried to make me give it to her. I'd die of embarrassment if anyone besides Amir read my poem.

"Give James his note and let me hear no more of this."

Barker turned back to the blackboard and wrote more fractions. I handed Bird my poem. At least he wouldn't tear it up, and he never read anything unless he had to. I almost hollered at him when he scrunched it in his back pocket, leaving part of the paper sticking out. I saw T.T. eyeing it. Mickey leaned over to me again. "That ain't really Bird's note. Who'd write him?"

"Why don't you mind your business, Mickey?" I mumbled. I nervously watched Bird's pocket and my poem and tried to get his attention so he'd pass the paper back to me. He was furiously erasing. I tried to concentrate on the numbers and keep track of my poem at the same time. It seemed as if every time I looked away from my paper or the blackboard, Barker saw me. Finally, she said, "Doris, do the next problem."

As I walked to the blackboard, I saw T.T. pass a piece of paper to the boy sitting alongside of him. Seemed like every pair of eyes in the room was pasted on my back. I didn't hear any talking, but I knew someone was sure to say something about my out-of-style pleated blue skirt or the way my hair was braided.

I finished the problem and walked quickly back to my desk. When I sat down, I saw that the paper wasn't in Bird's pocket. My blood went cold when I heard giggles and whispers throughout the room. I tried to act as though nothing were wrong, but I couldn't help looking in horror as I watched my poem going from hand to hand. A boy sitting next to Russell blew kisses at me. My hands shook as I copied another problem. I'd destroy Bird. Wring his scrawny neck. I twisted in my seat again to see where my poem was.

Mickey tapped me and handed me a wrinkled piece of paper.

"The one, the only Amir. With all my love, Doris," she said breathlessly, fluttering her eyelashes.

I snatched my poem out of her hand and stuffed it back into my notebook. "I'm getting you for this, Mickey."

They'd stolen my words. My eyes began to water, but I couldn't let the tears spill over. I leaned over my notebook and scribbled in the margins. I didn't care if Barker checked my book either. The worst thing had already happened. Nothing could be more embarrassing than everybody seeing your personal and private thoughts.

"Class, finish the problems and then take out your readers for silent reading. Turn to page 21." The teacher sat down at her desk, arranged a stack of papers, and started writing.

I opened the book and didn't care what page it was. I stared at blurry words running together, too ashamed to raise my head.

I didn't look up until the lunch bell rang, and I saw Bird reaching in his pockets and rummaging through his desk. I stood on the back of the line. Mickey, Dotty, Lavinia, and a couple other girls were at the head of the line whispering and giggling. It felt as if everyone in the room was laughing at me, and I couldn't look anyone in the eye.

I couldn't even go near the cafeteria. I sneaked to the schoolyard and sat on the steps while everyone ate lunch.

It wasn't until the end of the day that Bird came over to me as we walked down the hall to go home. "Doris, I can't find your note."

"Don't say nothing to me, Bird. I'm two minutes away from the side of your head. You let them get their hands on my poem."

He had the nerve to look at me like he didn't know what I was talking about.

"Who got your poem?" He looked confused.

"Don't give me any more help, Bird. All you did was make things worse!" I left him and ran downstairs. When I got outside, I raced across Cauldwell Avenue, took the shortcut through the playground, and didn't stop until I got to Miss Bee's.

# 3

The best thing about Miss Bee's Beauty Hive was the comforting sweet shampoo smell. I also loved the two posters of women with beautiful hairdos that stood in the tiny window next to the drooping spider plant. I wondered whether anyone ever came out of Miss Bee's with their hair looking like the women in the posters.

The Beauty Hive was small and narrow. More pictures of hairstyles were pasted on the walls. Three booths in the front of the shop were separated by the kind of thick frosty glass that you can't see through.

Miss Bee sat on a stool in the first booth, holding a large black curling iron over her customer's head. The other booths were empty. I almost tripped over a hair dryer cord.

"Who's that?" Miss Bee peeped above the top of the divider. "Hi, Honey Bunch," she said as soon as she saw me. A gleam of light sparkled out of her front gold tooth.

"Hi, Miss Bee," I said. "I just wanted —"

"Your mother sent you here to make an appointment for her? It's about time." She looked at her customer in the mirror. "You should see this child's mama. Pretty as a picture. But I lost her when she started wearing them out-of-date Afros."

If I didn't want a job so bad, I would've told her off. "My mother just like to be natural," I said.

She clicked the irons like castanets. "Natural? People wearing curls these days. That's what's natural now. So Honey Bunch, when does she want her appointment?"

"Miss Bee . . . I want to know if . . . I mean, do you —? I need a job."

"You and a lot of other people," she said. The customer laughed. Miss Bee's gold tooth glittered. "Yes, child. It's a rough world out there. Everyone's looking for work."

"Miss Bee . . . I mean . . . I was wondering if you need some help."

She twirled a lock of the customer's hair around the iron. "We all need help, Honey Bunch."

Smoke rose out of the customer's hair as Miss Bee made a big, fat curl. I moved from one foot to the other. I didn't know whether she was trying to be funny or really thought I had come in just to talk.

"Miss Bee, what I mean is, I was wondering whether you need someone to answer the phone, or run errands . . . or write down appointments. You know."

She put the irons in the burner and wiped her sweaty forehead. "Honey, I thought you was bringing some money in here. Not trying to take it out."

I was thinking of leaving right then until I thought about Amir upstate, and how sad we were both feeling, and how important it was for me to see him. "You don't need someone to keep things straight for you?"

Her counter, filled with lotions, shampoos, combs, brushes, curlers, and pins, looked worse than my table at home.

"You volunteering?"

"I mean when you're busy."

She looked around the empty shop. "Do it look busy in here?"

"Aren't Saturdays busy?"

"Well . . . sometimes, but I —"

"Miss Bee, I can braid hair too — and make all kinds of cornrows with beads and —"

She pulled the customer's hair with the iron so hard the lady squinched. "On no. My clientele don't want no braids. I ain't having no beads and all kind of crazy stuff walking out of my shop. I'd lose my customers."

"But Miss Bee, I —"

"You young people are backwards. We used to wear braids because we couldn't afford to go to the hairdresser. Right?" She looked at her customer, who agreed.

"Curls is what's happening now," she said, clicking the iron.

"But, Miss Bee, the little girls — I could braid their hair when they come in with their mothers."

"She shook her head. "Their mamas want those girls to have curls. When are you coming in for some? You a cute child. Let me curl your hair and you'll be a raving beauty."

The customer grinned, looking at me in the mirror. Miss Bee put the last curl in the woman's hair and slipped off her stool. "So child, I — Who is that fool?" She headed for the door, and I followed her.

Yellow Bird's face was pressed into the glass watching us. He looked like some kind of monster with his nose and lips mashed up against the window. I could have smacked him. Messing up my job interview.

"You know him?" Miss Bee asked.

"I think he lives around here."

"What you want, rascal?" she yelled, shaking her fist at Bird.

Bird ran. I'd tell him off good when I saw him. If I didn't get to see Amir, I didn't know what I'd do. I had to get this job. "Miss Bee, what about Saturday?"

Miss Bee wiped her hands on her apron and looked at me like I was wearing her out. "Come by then and see what's happening. Maybe you could run a few errands. Drop in."

"So I got the job?" I said excitedly as the customer handed her some money.

"If you want to call it that," Miss Bee said. "There are two other hairdressers here on Saturdays. They'll tip you for running to the store for them."

"Tip?"

"Yes. We all believe in helping the youth."

It wasn't what I'd expected, but it was better than nothing.

"I'll be here Saturday."

"Okay, honey. And tell your mama to come in for some curls."

Bird was gone when I got outside. Dotty was jumping double Dutch in front of her building with some little girls. Mickey and Lavinia were on the stoop, draped over the bannister like a pair of curtains. I was on the other side of the street but since the block is as narrow as the Beauty Hive, I know they all saw me. They didn't speak to me, though, and I didn't speak to them.

As I slowly walked up the stairs to my apartment, I wondered how I was going to break the news to Ma about my job. She should be happy since she's always telling me about responsibility. But she also hardly ever lets me out of her sight.

When I opened the door, I nearly bumped into her as she put on her jacket. "Doris, you ain't doing anything. I saw you walking up the block slow as a snail. Stay here with the baby for me while I run to Third Avenue to do some shopping. He's sleeping now."

Here was my chance to get on her good side. "I'll go for you, Ma."

"No. You can't shop like me. I'm looking for specials. Gotta save some money, you know. Be back soon."

I listened to her heels click down the hallway. After I heard the front door bang shut, I went to the kitchen to find a snack and checked on Gerald on my way to my room.

My room was really a hallway between my parents'

room and the rest of the apartment. It was only big enough for my bed and a monstrous old-fashioned chest of drawers that I used as both a dressing table and a desk. A small low bookcase stood under the window. I made a clearing on the top of the chest — barrettes, comb, and blouses to one side, books, papers, and pencils to the other. I did some homework for a while, and then took Amir's letter and the crumpled poem out of my notebook. I read them over and over again. My stomach hurt as I thought of the whole class reading my personal poem. I wasn't sorry I wrote it, though. Maybe people in class would think I was the biggest fool in the world, but Amir would understand and he'd feel good. The next time I see Yellow Bird . . . I thought.

As soon as Ma walked in the door, Gerald started to cry. "Doris, go get that child and keep an eye on him while I fix supper," Ma called to me from the kitchen.

I went and got Gerald, and then ran around behind him as he tore around the house. I pulled him out from under the table as he grabbed for a piece of raw onion that must have fallen off Ma's cutting board. I sat down at the table across from her with Gerald on my lap as she diced onions.

"Ma," I began, wincing as the smell of onion stung my nose. "What do you think about — ?"

The doorbell rang.

"Get that, Doris," Ma said, as she dropped potatoes into a pot of boiling water.

With Gerald in my arms, I went to the living room

and opened the door. Mrs. Nicols, who lived in the apartment upstairs, floated in with a big false-tooth smile. Once a week she came downstairs to visit Ma.

Mrs. Nicols and I sat at the table, and I sat Gerald next to me making sure he didn't splatter the walls with orange juice.

"Have some coffee?" Ma asked Mrs. Nicols. "Just put up a fresh pot on the stove."

"Yes, darling."

Ma handed her a water glass full of coffee. That was the only way she drank it. Once I asked Ma why Mrs. Nicols didn't drink coffee out of a cup like everyone else. Ma said, "Because she's not like everyone else."

Mrs. Nicols crossed her skinny legs and smiled at me. "Doris, you're a wonderful little mother's helper."

Ma put the onions into the frying pan, and she put a lid over the steaming pot of potatoes. "She's a good girl," Ma said. "Been real responsible lately."

Now was the time to say something about the job if I could get a chance to open my mouth.

Mrs. Nicols sipped her coffee loudly and put the glass on the table. If I'd have done that, Ma would have yelled.

She reared back in her seat and dangled her hands over the back of the chair. They were wrinkly and old, but her fingernails were long and pretty, sparkling with red nail polish. She reminded me of an older Lavinia. Mrs. Nicols hands spread like a fan, which meant that a speech was coming.

"This girl is precious," she said. "It's a cruel, vicious world out there. And there's no love like a mother's love, darling. Keep her close to home."

Ma smiled proudly as she gave the sizzling onions a stir. Ma said, "Yes. Doris is a good kid. And it ain't easy raising children nowadays. You have to watch them all the time."

I wished Mrs. Nicols would go back upstairs. She put her hand out as if she were waiting for someone to hand her something. "Girl, don't talk. You know, when I was a young lady, you went from your father's jurisdiction to your husband's."

She smiled, and even though she was old, something young happened to her face. "But, of course, I always had my own mind. Made sure I saw some of what happened between Daddy's house and my husband's house, God rest both their souls." She winked at Ma and picked up her coffee glass, her pinkie standing straight out like a soldier.

"These women liberationists need to come and see me," she continued. "I was a feminist long before they had a name for it."

Ma laughed at Mrs. Nicols' chatter. Maybe I'd say I was a feminist, too. That's why I wanted a job, I thought to myself. I wiped Gerald's mouth, still wondering how I could get one word between Mrs. Nicols' ten.

She took another long swallow of coffee and turned to my mother. "Talking about trouble youngsters get into, some of these old folks round here worse than kids. For instance, have you heard what folks around here saying about that woman upstairs on the top floor?"

Ma looked at me. "Doris, thanks for helping with Gerald. You can go and finish your homework now."

Now that Mrs. Nicols was getting to the good part of her visit, they wanted to get rid of me.

"Between me and Mrs. Nicols, we'll watch him." Ma gave me one of her fierce looks, and I knew I had to leave.

I heard Ma and Mrs. Nicols' voices in the kitchen while I tried to do my homework. Sometimes their voices would get really loud, and then they'd fade right when they got to the good part. They sounded like two young girls — gossiping and giggling. I wished Mrs. Nicols would hurry up and leave, but she didn't go until Daddy finally came home.

My father has the kind of face that looks like it's always crinkled in a laugh, but he came home an hour late, and his face was lined and tired. "I did the work of four men in that factory today," he complained as we all sat down at the dinner table.

Ma said, "When Gerald gets a little bigger, I'm going back to work."

"I want you to stay home with these kids," Daddy said, piling mashed potatoes and roast onto his plate. "I'll manage."

I sat up straight in my chair. "Suppose I get a job?"

Daddy didn't smile. "You already got one," he said. "Helping you mother."

Ma looked kind of amused. "Why do you want a job?" she asked.

"To make some money," I said.

She put a spoonful of mashed potatoes on my plate. "You're too young," she said and continued eating.

"Ma, I'm not too young," I said. "You always tell me I should be responsible."

Daddy stared at me. He still wasn't smiling. "We ain't that bad off. We give you everything you need," he said. "The junk you think you want ain't important."

"But, Daddy, I don't want to buy junk."

Ma rested her fork. "Doris, you better concentrate on your school. You have the rest of your lifetime to work, believe me."

"It won't interfere with school."

"No!" they both said at the same time. Daddy added, "You got work to do right here in this house." He patted my head like I was a puppy. "You stay in here and help your mother."

"But Daddy, suppose it was only on Saturdays?"

Ma didn't even let him answer. "We manage to give you any money you need for school, or to go out with your friends, and you ain't walking around in rags. We rich compared to half the people in this world," she said. "You working is a ridiculous idea. All we need is for the neighborhood to see us putting our eleven-year-old daughter to work," she continued.

"Can I have an allowance then?" I figured since we were so rich, they could give me a regular allowance.

Daddy wiped his mouth and put his napkin down. "Allowance?" he said. "You already get an allowance. I allow you to eat, sleep, and live here for free. That's your allowance. Allowance ain't nothing but bribery for getting a kid to do what she's supposed to do anyway. You live here. You part of this family. You supposed to help." He sounded exactly like my mother.

Ma didn't say a word and she even smiled a little. She always complained that Daddy was too soft with me, and I could tell she was glad to see him being tough.

I said no more. We ate quickly and quietly, and then they went to the living room to watch television. I washed and dried the dishes. It isn't fair, I thought. I wouldn't have a job or allowance. Even Mickey and Dotty get an allowance and there are two of them.

After I cleaned the kitchen, I stayed in my room for the rest of the evening. My parents never even asked what kind of job I was talking about. I sat at my table and stared at Amir's letter. Usually I did everything that Ma and Daddy told me to do, but they were wrong this time. It wasn't fair that Amir got taken away from his home on 163rd Street. And it wasn't fair that I lost my best friend. He only brought happiness and good things to everyone he was ever around, and now I was going to bring some happiness to him. I was going to visit him and cheer him up, and I was going to keep my job at the Beauty Hive. I'd prove to them that my going to work was a good idea.

# 4
## BIRD IN TROUBLE

BIRD IN TROUBLE

It was early, and the crisp morning air tingled like gingersnaps. 163rd Street was empty except for a few people going to the subway. I walked quickly to the mailbox across the street from school and slipped my letter to Amir inside. I added a P.S. to my letter to tell him I got a job with Miss Bee. I wished that I could know right then and there what he'd say when he found out I was getting a job so I could come and visit.

I crossed the street and headed toward the school entrance. As I walked up the steps I saw Bird, T.T., and Russell playing basketball in the yard. Bird made a hook shot that completely missed the basket, and T.T. and Russell got hysterical laughing at his silliness. I entered the building quickly so Bird wouldn't see me.

I headed straight for the library and sat in my usual spot by the window. Every time someone came through the doorway, I looked up from my book, hoping it wasn't Bird coming to bother me. When the bell rang, I adjusted my shoulder bag and walked slowly out of the library. I didn't want to face the rest of the day in class with my ex-friends.

"Hi, Doris. Let me help you carry all them books." Bird, sweating and holding a basketball, spotted me in the hallway and leaned up against the wall.

"I don't need your help."

He moved the basketball from one arm to the other and wiped his forehead with his sleeve. "You got all them books you carrying and that big shoulder bag. Here, let me help you."

I walked down the hall real fast. "Your help means trouble," I said.

"Aw, Doris, you still mad at me?" he said, sticking his head in my face.

I pushed him aside. "You need to be carrying your own books, instead of a basketball."

Bird was right on my heels when we entered the cafeteria. He bounced the ball hard and loud, and didn't stop until a teacher yelled at him.

Mickey's and Lavinia's mouths moved as soon as they saw me.

I stood on the end of the line, and Bird scooted behind me. Before he had a chance to say anything, the second bell rang and Mrs. Barker entered. She led us to our classroom, where a mysterious stranger stood waiting.

He was about six feet tall, had a perfect Afro, and the biggest smile with the prettiest teeth I ever saw. He didn't look like a parent or a teacher.

Everyone stopped talking when they saw him — except stupid T.T., who shouted, "Mrs. Barker, who's that?"

"Only two-year-olds point and yell," she said. "This *gentleman* is Mr. Washington. He is going to be conducting a special program at Dunbar Elementary."

The man smiled at us.

"Let's show Mr. Washington that we're ladies and gentlemen," Mrs. Barker said, staring daggers at T.T.

Everyone, except me, talked and whispered. I know Barker wanted to blow her top, but she had to be cool in front of Mr. Washington as he stood there next to her, checking us out.

"That's enough, class," she said. "Dunbar Elementary has been chosen as one of the schools to participate in a special program called Creative and Performing Arts in the Classroom. Professional artists, actors, musicians, writers, poets, and playwrights will spend time in the school throughout the year so you'll have first-hand knowledge about these arts. However, we're still involved with our regular work."

I *knew* he was someone different.

"Mr. Washington has written and directed plays, and he'll be with us for the entire year. He'll be conducting a drama club." She smiled at him, trying so hard to look and sound sweet. She stretched her arms toward us like some Broadway star. "Mr. Washington, they're all yours now."

He put his hands in his pockets and smiled again. As soon as he got to the front of the room, Barker stood by the doorway with her arms folded, looking just like her old general self.

"I'll explain a little bit about the program," he said. "And then I'd like to hear from you guys. I want you to participate so I'll know who you are and where you're coming from." His voice reminded me of smooth, thick ice cream. He told us we'd be writing and acting in our own plays. Then we'd have a big play that we'd put on at Christmas for the school and all the parents. I wished he was our teacher. Even Bird paid attention.

"And now, class," Mr. Washington said, resting his foot on the seat of a chair. "Who can tell me what the word *improvise* means?"

Lavinia's hand shot up before anyone else had a chance. She waved her red fingernail hands in the air to make her bracelets jingle. She didn't care whether she knew the answer or not, as long as she was seen and heard. "Doesn't it have something to do with acting?" she said proudly. Everybody knew it had something to do with acting.

"In a way." Mr. Washington wrote the word on the board. "*Improvise* means to create on the spot — to act or speak without notes or a script. Mrs. Barker told me that you're studying ancient Egypt. Suppose I said let's improvise a scene about one of the famous pharaohs? You'd have to know your history. Which means you did your reading and studying."

Bird jumped out of his seat. "Mr. Washington. Can we impro-impro — ?"

"James Towers, sit down!" Barker came back to normal.

Mr. Washington laughed. "It's okay. I like his enthusiasm."

"Something tells me there are some real stars in this class." He looked at Bird. "Young man who wants to improvise . . . James, right?"

Bird nodded. "Most people call me Bird," he said.

Mrs. Barker cleared her throat. "Mr. Washington is not one of your little pals. Your proper name is James."

"Well, James, alias Bird, come on up here. We're going to do some improvisation."

Bird scrambled out of his seat so fast he almost fell.

"Any more volunteers?" Mr. Washington stared at me. "How about you, young lady?"

He took me by surprise. "Ah . . . I . . . I . . ."

Mr. Washington's eyes looked soft and kind when he smiled.

"I can't act," I mumbled.

"There are other aspects of the theatre arts besides acting," he said. "There's directing, lighting, writing, staging. . . ."

"Oh" was all I said. I might like to learn about writing plays — but that didn't interest me half so much as my plans to see Amir.

"I want to act," Bird called from the front of the room.

"Okay, let's start," Mr. Washington said, walking over to Bird. "Who else wants to improvise with us?"

Most of the class stood up, except me and a few other people.

"We need a dramatic situation to build on. We're going to create a one-act play on the spot," Mr. Washington said excitedly, interrupting my thoughts. He turned to everybody who had gotten up and now stood in the front of the room with him. "We need a suggestion for a scene."

Bird was staring at the ceiling, then he snapped his fingers. "Hey, suppose two boys are lost?"

"That sounds like you and T.T.," a girl called out.

Bird, Lavinia, and the rest of them acted out a scene about lost boys and a town bully. Bird was so good, I believed he was really that lost boy. They did some more scenes, and Bird took over the lead in all of them. There was so much laughing, I guess they were having a good time, but I didn't pay them any mind. I just wished that Amir were still here and things was like they used to be.

When the lunch bell rang, everyone groaned and sighed. Dotty said, "We have to go?"

"Time flies when you're having fun," Mr. Washington said.

Suddenly they all acted so silly, tumbling over each other as they went to the clothing closet and then lined up. T.T. yanked a handful of Lavinia's braids and she yelled. Instead of walking to the closet like a normal person, Bird jerked his body stiffly like electric shocks ran through his toothpick arms and legs.

Mrs. Barker looked mad, but Mr. Washington looked so amazed that Barker didn't say anything. "What do you call that dance?" Mr. Washington asked.

"Electric Boogey," T.T. yelled, trying to do the same dance, but he couldn't move like Bird.

"James is a great dancer," Mr. Washington said.

Bird really got bold. That was all he needed to hear. He did The Moonwalk—sliding backwards right under Barker's nose while she glared at him. If looks could kill, Bird would've been a dead duck.

"Class, quiet," Mrs. Barker said through clenched teeth, trying not to yell. "Mr. Washington has an announcement to make."

"It's been wonderful meeting you. You kids are talented and I expect to see all of you on Monday. I'll be in the auditorium signing up people for the Drama Club." He turned to Mrs. Barker and shook her hand. "I enjoyed your class, and especially that little character over there in the red sweatshirt."

Bird grinned a 200-watt smile.

"Thank you for coming," she said, smiling stiffly. She cut her eyes at Bird who started dancing again, sliding all the way to the back of the room.

He walked to the door and looked back at us again. "Remember, everyone can join," he said. His eyes caught mine, and I looked away. I didn't want to be in any club. When I saw Amir, we'd be our own club.

The class all babbled at once. "I'll be the first one there," Bird shouted from the back of the room. I never saw him so enthusiastic before.

"Where he say to join up?" someone else yelled.

Mr. Washington waved to us and left the room. Barker closed the door behind him, and like thunder follows lightning, I knew an explosion was coming. People were so excited about acting, they forgot they was in a classroom.

"Sit down!" she yelled.

Everyone scrambled to their desks—even me, who hadn't done anything. Mrs. Barker paced back and forth. "After behaving so well and having so much fun this morning, you have to act like this."

T.T. poked Bird in his back and giggled. Why do Bird and the rest of them have to show off so much and make us all late for lunch?

"And you, James," Barker continued, pointing at Bird. "I'm not so sure you'll be joining that club unless you knuckle down and bring up your grades. Or *you*, T.T."

T.T. shrugged his shoulders. "I wasn't joining no way," he mumbled.

Bird bounced out of his seat. "I've got to join, Mrs. Barker," Bird pleaded. "I'll be good. I've got to join. Please?"

"Extracurricular activities are a privilege, not a right. And one doesn't earn the privilege by cutting up like you do. Now sit down!"

Bird kept walking toward her, his arms outspread. Someone giggled.

Nobody but Bird would have messed with Barker now. Especially if they wanted something from her.

"Mrs. Barker, I promise I'll do better. I —"

She was getting red as a lobster. "How do you intend to spend time in a club when you're failing everything except recess? Now sit down."

Russell let out a rude laugh. Now, I began to feel a little sorry for Bird. I could tell how much he wanted to join that club. And she shouldn't have told him he was failing everything in front of the whole class.

Bird was mad. "You got to let me join, Mrs. Barker," he said desperately.

"If you're not in your seat in one second, you're not joining anything."

Bird walked past her to the door. She lunged after him, but he was too fast for her. He left the room and slammed the door — in her face.

Everyone gasped. No one ever walked out of the room, slamming the door in Mrs. Barker's face. She was so angry she stopped raging.

"Everyone on line," she said. "Quietly."

No one said a word as we marched silently down the hall behind her. When we reached the cafeteria, she told us that Bird was getting suspended. She left us and headed in the direction of the principal's office.

Russell watched her stomp down the hall. "Bird's really in trouble now," he said.

Everyone was dead quiet.

My no-fail plan began smoothly on Saturday. When I finished my chores, I told Ma that I was going outside to play. All she said was, "Be in before dark." Since I had no friends, I didn't have to worry about anyone coming to my house looking for me, and Daddy would be at work. Ma would be in the house with Gerald, so they could never find me at Miss Bee's.

As I walked down the street past the empty lot, I saw Mrs. Nicols stepping quickly by the Beauty Hive. Her little feathered hat was cocked to the side of her head. The feather bobbed each time she stepped. She'd ask a million questions if she saw me going into the Hive. I relaxed when she disappeared around the corner.

The usual cloud of smoke rose out of Miss Bee's booth as she curled another customer's hair. There was a lady under the dryer and another woman was in the back having her hair washed. Two other customers sat in chairs reading fashion magazines as they waited to have their hair done. A hairdresser was in the booth next to Miss Bee's.

"Hi, Honey Bunch!" She seemed surprised to see me, like she forgot I was coming.

"Hi, Miss Bee. I'm here to help out."

Miss Bee looked puzzled.

"Remember, you said I could come today?"

"Oh, yes. Yes. Things are a little slow. You can observe, so you learn something about the business of beauty." Her gold tooth gleamed.

"Miss Bee, I —"

"This is the little lady I was telling you about, girls," she called to the other hairdressers. How could she be telling them about me when she forgot I was coming? I wondered.

The young, pretty hairdresser in the last booth was putting curlers in her customer's hair. "Hi," she said to me, "my name's Carol. You want to learn about beauty, honey? Come on and pull up a chair."

Miss Bee said, "If she wants to learn about beauty, then she's pulling up to the wrong booth." Everybody laughed, including Carol. There was another hairdresser in the back, washing someone's hair. She looked over at me. "That child don't look like she want to be no hairdresser. She's going to college."

I wondered how she knew that, since she'd never seen me before. Then one of the women who was waiting said, "Women can do other things these days besides hairdressing, nursing, teaching, and wifing."

Miss Bee clicked her curling iron. "Don't start talking about wifing and husbands again." They all joked and teased while I stood there feeling out of place, waiting for someone to tell me what to do.

People came in and out. A man walked in selling perfume. "Ladies, add some sweetness to your life," he said.

Miss Bee said, "Junior, the sweetest thing could happen to us is you leave."

A woman came in selling little glass animal figurines. "They don't make this kind of stuff anymore," she said.

Miss Bee looked at the figurines so hard I thought they'd turn to ash. "They don't make horse and buggies anymore either, darling," she said. There was more laughing and I just stood there, probably looking stupid.

Finally, Carol said to me, "Take these papers off the rollers and separate the pink, blue, and yellow ones." She handed me two bags full of rollers. After I did that, the other hairdresser asked me to fold some towels for her.

I finished that real fast and then I had nothing to do. There's nothing more boring than sitting around a place — especially when everyone else is busy. I sat down near Carol's booth again, looking around for something to keep me busy.

"Do you know how much it would cost to go to Syracuse?" I asked.

"Why on earth would anyone want to go there?" Miss Bee called out from her booth.

"No reason. I just wondered," I said. "I have a friend there."

"My sister lives upstate," Carol said. "It might run you around fifty dollars."

My heart fell when I heard that. I'd never earn that much. I had to get busy at Miss Bee's.

Later, a woman with a little girl came in to have her hair done. The little girl looked at me, and I smiled back at her. "Hi, cutie," I said. "How old are you?"

Her bright, round eyes sparkled. "Five," she answered.

"She'd look real pretty with a nice cornrow-design hairstyle," I said to her mother. Miss Bee shot me a look. I was only expressing my opinion.

The little girl's mother said, "Can you do it?"

"Sure. I can cornrow." I couldn't lie and say no. I *do* know how to cornrow.

"Good. You braid her hair while I get mine done. Keep her quiet for a while."

It seemed like a tremendous mushroom cloud of smoke rose out of Miss Bee's booth, but she didn't say a word, except, "Times do change." I fixed the girl's hair in a circular design. It looked beautiful, if I must say so myself. Miss Bee knew it looked good too, though she wouldn't admit it to me. The girl's mother gave me $3.00.

After I finished the girl's hair, Miss Bee asked me to clean her counter and get out the sprays, gels, and combs and irons so she'd be ready for the next customer. I did that and then she asked me to water that sickly spider plant in the window.

As I climbed onto the window ledge and watered the plant I realized that I was standing right in the window. I hurried before anyone I knew walked by and saw me. The kids, as usual, were running up and down playing. I didn't notice anyone else. The telephone rang.

"Honey Bunch, answer that," Miss Bee hollered from her booth.

I put on the most adult voice I could find. "Beauty Hive," I said. "It's for you Miss Bee: a lady wants an appointment."

"Take it for me," she said, pointing to the table. "There's my book."

I picked up the phone again. "When would you like an appointment? Next Saturday at four?"

"Check my book and see what I have open for Saturday," Miss Bee yelled.

"Excuse me," I said, "let me check her appointment book." I rested the phone and looked through the book. Miss Bee, you got a Mrs. Brown coming at four."

"Okay. See if the lady can come at five. I try to schedule them an hour apart."

"Can you come at five?" I said to the customer. "Okay, that's October 31st, at five o'clock." I hung up the phone and wrote the appointment in her book.

The phone rang again, and I really showed out this time. "Good afternoon, Miss Bee's Beauty Hive. Can I help you? Yes. When would you like the appointment? One o'clock Tuesday? Let me check, hold on, please. . . . Okay, Mrs. Jones. You have an appointment for one o'clock next Tuesday. Good-bye."

"Very nice, Honey Bunch," Miss Bee said. "You make a good little receptionist. Bring some class to this joint."

The next time the phone rang, I made an appointment for Carol. The Hive was buzzing. People were coming and going. Every chair in the place was taken — even the one I sat in, by Carol's booth. For all Miss Bee's scheduling, she had two people waiting for her. All three dryers were occupied. Curling irons were clicking. And everytime the phone rang I answered it. That was my job. I was truly a part of what was happening.

The phone rang again and my voice sang out, "Good afternoon, Miss Bee's Beauty Hive. Can I help you?"

"Doris, girl, that you? You better bring your hind parts home this minute." The song left my voice, and my throat closed up.

"Yes, Ma. I'll be right there," I whispered.

"Who was that, Honey Bunch?"

I tried to keep my voice from trembling. "It was the wrong number. What time is it, Miss Bee? My mother said I shouldn't be too late."

"It's four thirty. Things'll be slowing down soon." She dug down in her pocket. "You was a good help. See you next Saturday." She handed me $5.00.

"Thank you, Miss Bee," I said softly.

I started putting on my jacket. Carol said, "Here, baby. You a nice girl and smart, too." She gave me $2.00.

The other operator wiped her hands on her smock. "Yeah. It's nice having you around. A real little lady. Know how to follow directions too. Some of these kids, you tell 'em turn left and they go right." She gave me

$2.00 also. I couldn't tell them that my career at the Hive was probably over. "See you next week," I said softly as I walked out.

"Tell your mama to come in for some curls," Miss Bee called after me.

My mama's hair is probably already curled I thought to myself as I walked slowly up 163rd Street to my building.

# GROUNDED

When I walked into the kitchen, all Ma said was, "Girl!" Her eyes and mouth turned to slits. I put my hands up to my face, but she didn't slap me.

Daddy's whole face was a frown. He sat at the table holding Gerald. Ma stood by the sink, folding her arms. "What was you doing hanging out, in of all places, the Beauty Hive?" she yelled.

"Ma, I wasn't hanging out." I let the tears roll.

She walked over to Daddy and sat down next to him. He still wasn't saying anything.

"Them crocodile tears ain't gonna help nothing, Doris," Ma said. "Now tell us what was you doing in there." Poor Gerald, between her yelling and my tears, started crying too.

"Mrs. Nicols said she couldn't believe her eyes when she was passing by and saw you in the window watering that dead plant," Ma continued.

I wiped my eyes with a fist like a big dumb kid. Daddy handed me his handkerchief. "I was just . . . just helping Miss Bee out . . ." I sobbed. "I wanted to earn some money . . . that's all. I wasn't doing nothing wrong."

"Wasn't doing nothing wrong? Me and your father told you that you wasn't to go out and get a job. You ignored us and went out of this house like a grown woman."

I sat silently.

Daddy's voice sounded heavy, like a foghorn. "Doris, your mother lets you go out and play on Saturdays when she could really use you in here to help her." He drummed his hand on the table. "If you so itchy to work, you stay in this house and help your mother."

Ma stood up and started making coffee. "You're grounded, Doris," she said. "You ain't gonna see them streets except for school and back."

"You're *not* to go to work outside this house," Daddy said and plopped Gerald in his high chair and left the kitchen. He seemed even angrier than Ma, even though she the one who done the punishing.

Ma turned up the gas under the coffee. "You defiantly disobeyed us, Doris. There's dangers outside this house, and we can't have you running around like some wild child doing things we don't permit."

"I'm sorry, Ma," I said. I started feeling bad that I'd disobeyed them. I didn't mean to hurt them. "I still don't see why you all don't want me to work," I said.

"You father doesn't even want me to go back to work right now. He wants me to be home with you and Gerald." She stared at the coffeepot.

"Why? You worked this summer," I said.

"That was an emergency and you were home from school." She tapped her arm with her fingers as she watched the pot.

Ma turned the coffee off and poured herself a cup. "Your father is a very proud man, Doris." She sat down across from me. "He doesn't want his young daughter out there working as if he can't take care of his family." She took a sip of coffee. "You are too young — just turned eleven. You can work when you're a teenager."

"I can't wait that long, Ma," I said. "Anyway, don't you like Miss Bee?"

"She's all right. Hardworking woman. Smart enough to hold on to her own business all these years. But, Doris, the problem is not whether or not I like Miss Bee. The problem is, your father and I aren't sending our child out to work. And besides, you're too young to be hanging around them women in the beauty parlor all day."

"You used to let me go there to get my hair done," I reminded her.

"That was only on special occasions. You wasn't in there all day. Besides, that woman don't change with the times. People come out of her shop looking like a French poodle."

She handed Gerald his teddy bear. "What about your schoolwork?"

"The job is only on Saturdays. It won't interfere with school."

"Doris, how much money you say you made?"

"I didn't say. Twelve dollars — I know it ain't a lot but . . ."

She leaned back in the chair and crossed her legs. You could put a dime in her dimples when she smiles. "Doris, that money ain't taking us from rags to riches. Like Mrs. Nicols said, you need to be close to home."

I wished Mrs. Nicols wouldn't talk so much. "I am close to home. The Hive is just down the block."

"That ain't close enough. And don't keep bugging me about that job, which ain't no real job anyway." She took another sip of coffee. "You in that shop all day and all she paid you is twelve dollars?"

"That was tips I made."

She looked up at the ceiling. "Please. She ain't even paying wages."

"Ma, I made a beautiful cornrow design for a little girl."

Ma stared into space for a minute and smiled to herself. "You and your girl friends been cornrowing from the time you played with dolls."

"But I do it good now. The lady paid me three dollars." Ma was surprised, but she tried not to show it.

I squeezed her arm. "Ma, did you know that cornrowing came from ancient Africa? I read about it in a book. Every style has a meaning, Ma, and —"

"What does that have to do with working at the Hive?"

"I'd be practicing an ancient African art right in the Beauty Hive."

"You practice your ancient African art in this apartment."

"How long am I grounded?"

"Two weeks."

"Ma!" I couldn't even go back to Miss Bee's if I wanted to. My plans were totally ruined. "Ma, that's too long," I said.

"You lucky it ain't longer," she said, taking Gerald out of his high chair. She carried the baby out of the kitchen and I stared at the four walls. I'd *really* messed up this time. Somehow, I had to come up with a new plan.

On Monday, Bird wasn't at school, and by lunch time, everyone was talking about his suspension. I didn't think it was fair — especially since he had been trying so hard to get serious. I sat at the far end of the lunch table, away from my ex-friends so I could figure out how to convince my mother to let me keep my job with Miss Bee. But I couldn't get away from all of their talk.

Russell took a big bite out of his baloney sandwich. "Wonder when Bird's father or mother will bring him back to school so he can get off suspension," he said.

"He's probably been grounded for the next five months," Mickey piped in. Bird ain't the only one grounded, I said to myself.

Lavinia leaned back in her seat and fingered one of the beads in her hair. "That Yellow Bird picked a fine time to mess up. We have the first Drama Club meeting today."

Dotty jumped out of her seat and tried to imitate Bird's dance.

"That club went to his fool head," Russell said.

"The class ain't no fun without him," T.T. added.

"This is a schoolhouse, not a funhouse, T.T.," Lavinia said waving her hand at him like she was shooing a fly. She turned her back to him to talk to Mickey and Dotty. T.T. stood behind her, imitating the way she moved her head from side to side while she talked. "Mr. Washington says I have talent, and he said Bird is good too. Isn't Mr. Washington fine?"

It's a wonder Mickey and Dotty didn't break their necks nodding at every word that came out of Lavinia's mouth.

Bird was out of school for the rest of the week, and I was beginning to worry about him. I have to admit I enjoyed the peace and quiet, and I was still a little bit mad at him for what he'd done with my poem. Still, I wondered what had happened to him.

When school ended on Friday, I rushed home to see if I'd gotten a letter yet from Amir. On the way, I thought of my new plan of action to get off punishment and convince Ma why I needed to keep my job at Miss Bee's.

Ma had always told me that if you do good things, good things will come back to you. For the whole week, good became my middle name. One evening, while setting the table without being reminded, Ma said, "This wonderful behavior must be for a reason." I guess she knows me pretty well.

When I got home, Ma was sitting at the kitchen table, reading the paper.

"Ma?" I said, as I entered the kitchen.

"What, Doris?" she said without looking up from her paper.

"Did I get a letter?"

"No." She continued reading.

"Ma, you remember my friend Amir?"

She looked up and stared at me closely. "Yes. And I've been meaning to talk to you about that." She put down her mail and walked over to the stove to heat a pot of coffee. When she puts that coffee on, that means a long serious talk is coming. Why did I open my big mouth?

"I notice you been down in the mouth since your friend left. Maybe that has something to do with this job business?"

She poured the steaming coffee in her cup and sat down at the table. "I had a good friend once. We was like sisters. I thought I'd never find another buddy when she moved. Even started hating the friends I had because they wasn't like her." She stirred the coffee. "But life goes on and your life is here."

"What if I went to visit him, Ma?" I asked hesitantly.

She gazed at me like she was looking at something strange. "Do you think we'd let you go all the way upstate alone to see a boy?"

"We're best friends. He's not just a boy."

"You got a whole block full of best friends right here on 163rd Street. Discussion closed." She picked up her coffee and went to the living room.

Even though I knew Ma meant what she'd said, I

still fantasized on Saturday morning that at any moment she would come up to me and tell me that I was off punishment and could keep my job. I even put out the garbage without being asked and cleaned the living room, which wasn't one of my regular Saturday chores. I called her to look at my work. "Ma, how do you like that?"

Everything was polished to a high shine. She folded her arms. "Okay, Doris. What do you want?"

"Am I still grounded?"

"I told you two weeks."

"Ma, I'm sorry for what I did. I was doing it for us — for the family. I thought you'd be proud when I came home with money I earned with my own hands. And I —"

She sighed. "Stop whining and lying. You know you was just trying to make money to go see your friend. I'll let you off, but you better not go near that beauty parlor."

"I have to tell Miss Bee that I can't help her."

"You had all week to tell her."

"But I was grounded. You told me to come straight home from school."

"Doris, don't play with me. You go over there and tell her that you cannot work for her and that's all you do."

"Yes, Ma," I mumbled. "Then can I go to the movies?"

"I don't have the money. Them movies just junk anyhow."

"Then why can't I work?"

"Don't start up again with that job nonsense, Doris." She turned on the television. "What about your own money?"

I smiled. "Oh no. I'm saving that, since I can't work. I don't know when I'll have so much money again." I put on my jacket. "Ma, the mail come today yet?"

"No. I wish you'd stop bugging me about the mail. And don't roam the Bronx."

I walked slowly down 163rd Street toward the Beauty Hive, dodging the little children playing stickball on the street. I didn't want to tell Miss Bee I couldn't come there anymore. I *had* to earn money to visit Amir. Things had been so good last week. Everything was perfect until Ma called.

The Hive was quiet and no cloud of smoke rose out of Miss Bee's booth. But as soon as I walked in, she said, "Honey, I'm glad to see you. I have a big job coming in here soon and I'm out of paper towels." The shop was empty. Not even the other hairdressers were around.

"Miss Bee, I —"

"The customer coming in is a bride-to-be. Getting married this evening and she's a nervous wreck." Miss Bee gave me $4.00. "Get four rolls of paper towels. Oh, and water that plant before you go."

"Miss Bee, I —"

"I always forget about that plant. What was you saying, Honey Bunch?"

"Miss Bee, I . . . that plant look dead to me."

"No, it ain't. It'll come back to life if we remember to water it."

I walked to the window. This was how I got caught before. But I was only doing her a favor . . . watering the plant and then going to the store. I wouldn't take money for it. I pulled the plant out of the window and took it to the back and watered it. I had to tell her. "Miss Bee, my mother said —"

The phone rang. "Let me get that, honey. Now you hurry back with them towels."

How was I supposed to quit my job if Miss Bee wouldn't let me talk?

I hesitated at the door and then stepped quickly outside. As I crossed 163rd Street, I heard a familiar, "Yo, Doris!"

"Bird. I ain't seen you since you been suspended," I said.

He made a silly face and started dancing on the street. "I've been making my debut on Broadway," he joked. "I just saw your mother. Asked me if I knew where you was."

I closed my eyes. Oh, no. If she saw me running an errand for Miss Bee, she'd think I was still working. She'd put me back on punishment until I was twenty. "Where was she?" I asked.

"Going to the store on Third Avenue."

I stopped walking.

"Why you look so upset, Doris? You still mad at me?"

At first I didn't know what he was talking about. He

didn't wait for me to answer. Seems like no one was letting me talk.

"What did I miss in school last week? Is Barker still mean? Is Russell still big? Is —"

"Bird, will you quit talking?" I walked toward my building. Here I am in desperate trouble, and he's bugging me about school.

"Where you going? The twins and them went to the candy store."

I sucked my teeth. "I don't care about where the twins and them went."

"You still mad huh?" he said. "It was T.T. who stole your note." He sat next to me on the stoop. "I was only trying to help you that day."

"Bird, you can help me by leaving me alone."

"Come on, Doris, don't be like that." He kicked a rock into the gutter. "Say you ain't mad at me no more." He poked his bottom lip out like a baby fixing to cry.

I smiled, even though I didn't want to.

"Say you ain't mad no more." He grabbed me by the shoulders.

"Bird, please." I pushed him away.

"I'll do anything to hear you say it. Let me do something nice for you." He stood up. "What you want? Just say, 'Bird, I forgive you.' " He clutched his hands to his heart. A woman walking by saw him and smiled. "Doris, I'll do anything for you. Just say 'I forgive.' "

"Bird, you silly, and you getting on my nerves."

He sat down again. "Well, at least you talking to me. Come on, Doris, let me help you with something — anything, okay? Let me carry your books for you." He grinned, "I'd do your homework for you too, except it'd be wrong, but I'd do it."

"You making me smile when I don't want to smile, Bird. I want to think."

"Let me help you. There must be —"

"Could you go to the store for me?" Soon as the question left my mouth I was sorry I asked it. How could I ask Bird to do something important?

"Yeah. You can't leave the block?"

"It's a long story. Think you can do it without messing up?"

"How could I mess up going to the store?"

"You know how you are. And don't tell nobody you going for me." He looked at me real strange when I handed him the money and told him what I wanted.

Soon as he left, I started worrying. Suppose he came back with the wrong thing? Four rolls of toilet tissue or four boxes of Kleenex. Suppose he lost the money? I began to think that sending Bird to the store might have been the dumbest idea I ever had. I wished Bird would hurry.

I didn't foresee what happened next. Bird walked down one end of 163rd Street, and my mother down the other. Ma peeped in the Hive when she passed it. Luckily, she got to me first, because Bird stopped to talk to some little boys that were playing on the street.

"I was looking for you to go to the store for me," Ma said.

I frowned and shook my head slightly as Bird started walking toward us carrying a large bag.

"Where was you?" she asked.

"I went around the corner. . . ." I wished she'd hurry upstairs. Bird was still walking toward us. Ma had her back to him. She was smiling at the kids playing stickball on the street and looking around like this was the first time she'd laid eyes on 163rd Street.

I stared at Bird, then rolled my eyes toward my mother. He looked slightly confused, but he must have understood because he stopped walking. Holding the large package tightly, he turned around and sat on his stoop.

"Ma, I'm going up the street, okay?"

"All right. Don't let me have to come and look for you."

When she went in the building, I raced over to Bird. "Thank you," I said as I took the package and the change. "Bird, you saved me. I was almost under punishment for the rest of my life."

"Bird, where you been?" Russell yelled to him from the other side of the street. T.T. was with him.

"We going to the playground," T.T. said.

"You mean I did something good for you?" Bird said. "You mean I didn't get you into trouble?"

"You just got me out of a lot of trouble, Bird," I answered.

Bird grinned like he was tickled. I guess he doesn't do too many things right. "Then you forgive me?" he said. "And you ain't mad at me no more?"

"Well, I didn't exactly say that."

"Come on, Doris, say it. Say I. Forgive. You. Bird. I. Ain't. Mad. At. You. No. More."

I sighed. "Okay, Bird, I say both."

"Say it out. I forgive you, Bird."

"I forgive you, Bird."

"I ain't mad at you no more," he said.

"I ain't mad at you no more," I repeated.

Without any warning, Bird hugged me and almost knocked the package out of my hand. "See you around, friend," he said grinning, and then tore across the street to join Russell and T.T. while I went to the Hive.

Bird isn't all that bad. In fact he's beginning to grow on me some. I wondered why he didn't say anything about being suspended. Everything must have turned out okay for him, because he was acting like his old Bird self again. Maybe Barker was just trying to scare us.

When I got back to the Hive, Miss Bee's bride-to-be customer was already there. She looked almost as old as Miss Bee. Every kind of shampoo, dye, lotion, and conditioner was laid out on the counter. Like my mother would say, she had everything out except the snake oil.

Miss Bee was as excited as the bride. "Honey Bunch, I'm glad you back. Now, clean these for me." She handed me two brushes.

"Miss Bee, I don't think I . . ."

"Before you clean them brushes, Honey Bunch, take a look at this."

She held up her customer's hand for me to see her engagement ring. "Ain't this something? Dazzles just like the bride." Her customer grinned from ear to ear over Miss Bee's compliment, and Miss Bee chattered on about weddings and all about the two times that she was married.

How could I interrupt her now to tell her I wasn't coming back? I thought while I was cleaning the brushes. Miss Bee's stories were better than Mrs. Nicols's. And best of all, there was no one there to send me out of the room. After I finished, Miss Bee said, "Thank you, Honey Bunch." She reached in her smock pocket and handed me $2.00. "You was a good little helper. Don't know what I'd have done without you. Ain't no point in sitting around here all day, though. Things is quiet."

"Thank you, Miss Bee. I . . ." I tried to hand the money back to her, but she was putting some gooey white stuff in the woman's hair and she didn't see me.

"Yes, Honey Bunch?"

"Miss Bee. I —"

"I'll see you next week," Miss Bee said.

"I guess so," I said, wishing I'd had the nerve to tell her I wasn't coming back. I would have a week to figure out how to tell her, but Ma would be some kind of angry if she knew that I hadn't quit my job.

I put on my jacket and left. There seemed to be more kids on the block than before. A bunch of little girls played on Mickey and Dotty's stoop. I continued walking to my building and sat down on the steps. I touched the $2.00 in my pocket. I shouldn't have let her pay me. But now I had $14.00. Still a long way from the $50.00 I needed.

"Doris!"

I looked up to my window. "Glad you still there," Ma said. "I forgot to get milk. Get me a large container."

Ma wrapped the coins in a handkerchief and tossed it out the window. "And by the way," she yelled, "You got a letter from Amir."

I nearly fell off the stoop. "Let me read it before I go to the store." I started racing up the stairs.

"Go to the store first, Doris. I need that milk now."

Instead of going all the way to Third Avenue, I was going to go to the small grocery store on Union Avenue, which was closer. I couldn't wait to get upstairs to read Amir's letter.

"And Doris," Ma called after me. "Don't you go to the store on Union Avenue. It's too expensive."

After I bought the milk, I flew into the house and yelled, "Ma! Where's the letter?"

"Calm yourself, Doris," she said, taking the milk and counting up the change. She wiped her hands on her apron and handed me the letter. I dashed to my room, so that I could read in private.

October 29th

Dear Doris,

I was happy to get your beautiful poem and your letter. The colors of the leaves here in late October are more magnificent than anything I ever saw. Like someone with big buckets of red and orange paint splashed the trees. One day, I want to paint a picture of them myself.

I hope the other kids on the block ain't mad at me for not saying goodbye or telling them I was going. I thought I was used to not having real parents and being moved from place to place. But I guess I wasn't. It hurts leaving places, and I was real hurt when I had to leave 163rd Street — especially because I had to leave you, Doris.

I don't think it's a good idea for you to come and visit me up here just yet. It's hard to explain, but my counselor told me that I need to get used to being here by myself. I made some new friends here. It's not like 163rd Street, but everyone here is kind and friendly, and we live in small cottages that are each like little families. And best of all is I saw one of my brothers. We haven't seen each other in five years. He lives with a family that wants to adopt him. The Smiths. They said that even when they adopt him that they going to let us be close, like brothers.

Maybe when things get settled more here you can come and visit. But until then, we not really separated. You should help Bird again like we used to. That will help me feel good if you can do that for him. He once told me that the reason he played so much and acted so silly was because he didn't want people to know he couldn't read and do his school work so well. You got to see inside of Bird to see who he really is. I bet if you helped him, Doris, he'd be a good student. Remember how he was beginning to change?

Love,
Amir

I couldn't answer Amir's letter right away. I wasn't sure what to say. I thought he'd want me to come up right away. Instead, his letter made me feel sad, the way I felt when he'd just left. I wished that I could do something to cheer him up and to make the hurting in me go away, but Amir didn't need me now. He just needed to be alone and take care of himself. I put his letter under my pillow, and lay there staring at the peeling paint on the ceiling. I wondered what I could do right now to help cheer up Amir.

## 8

8

# YELLOW
YELLOW
# BIRD
BIRD
# AND ME
AND ME

There was a light knock on the classroom door as Mrs. Barker finished taking attendance Wednesday morning. She opened the door, and in walked Bird behind his father. He didn't look as happy as he did when I saw him on Saturday.

I'd seen Bird's father on the block sometimes. He never spoke much to anyone and looked like he'd get angry if you said hello. He was a tall version of Bird with the same light skin and long nose. His clothes kind of hung on him, too. I wondered why his mother didn't come. Then it occurred to me that I hadn't seen her since summer ended.

Barker tried to smile. "Let's go outside, Mr. Towers."

She turned to us. "Open your spellers and study your words for this week." Everyone was quiet. I guess we all wanted to hear what Barker was telling Bird's father. I didn't hear Bird's voice at all.

Suddenly his father yelled. Then came the sound of a big slap. It stung me. Seemed like the whole class stopped breathing. General Barker marched in the room. Bird followed her, his head nearly touching the floor. I felt sorry for him. Getting slapped in school by your parent was one of the worst things that could ever happen.

We had to write a composition for English. Usually Bird got himself a pass to leave the room when it was time to write. He picked up his pencil and notebook and scratched something on the paper. He spent most of the time staring at the topic on the board.

I was feeling real bad for Bird. Maybe Amir was right. Bird really did need help, even though he always seemed so silly. Hadn't he acted like nothing at all was wrong last time I saw him? If I'd just gotten suspended, I wouldn't have been out playing and acting the fool like I seen him do on Saturday. He'd been a friend to me then, and he kept me off punishment. Maybe it would be a long time before I could see Amir again. But if I could help Bird, Amir and me wouldn't be separated, because I'd be doing something that we used to do together.

Mrs. Barker peeped at Bird over her glasses, but she didn't say anything. I guess she was so happy Bird's father slapped him she decided to give him a break. I noticed T.T. whispering to Bird, but he ignored him.

Barker collected the compositions, and then we had our reading lesson. She called on people to read aloud. The boy sitting next to Russell volunteered. Bird's face was practically inside his book. I figured it was about time now for him to do something crazy to get himself thrown out of the room or ask for a pass to the bathroom.

When the boy finished reading, I raised my hand. After I read, Barker looked around. A lot of people raised their hands because it was an easy short story. Barker liked to catch people who looked like they wasn't prepared. Her eyes scanned the room, ignoring the waving hands. "James Towers," she called.

"Y-yes, Mrs. Barker?"

"Read the next paragraph."

Someone snickered. I wondered whether he'd do a tap dance or spin on his head. Anything but read aloud in class. He cleared his throat.

"The boy re-re —"

I began to feel so embarrassed for Bird I wished he'd act silly like he usually does when he doesn't know his work.

"Remembered," Barker called sharply.

"The boy rem — I mean, remembered to . . . to . . . look in his pac — I mean, poc —"

I tried to ignore what was happening to Bird, but I couldn't. I remembered how much he improved last year when Amir helped him.

"Pocket!" The boy behind me yelled.

"No calling out," Barker said. Then she looked at Bird. "See, this is the result of always playing around, young man!"

"Mrs. Barker, I wasn't playing. . . . I —"

Lavinia giggled loudly and shook her head.

"If you refuse to do the work, you'll be put out of this class."

Bird tried again. "The boy remem-remem —"

"You read that already," Barker sighed.

"Oh. I'm sorry." Then Bird just made up a whole paragraph that wasn't even in the book. A girl whispered loudly, "Oh brother."

The boy behind me said, "Dog, he can't read nothing."

Barker stopped Bird. "That's enough. You'd better get serious, young man. I'm not putting up with your foolishness much longer."

Other people continued reading. I thought of what Amir had said in his letter. This time Bird wasn't clowning. Seemed to me that he was trying to read. Barker just didn't understand him.

She stood at her desk. "Now, class, we'll form groups to study for the end of the unit social studies test. Those of you who want to study alone may do so."

Lavinia raised her hand right away. "Me, Mickey, and Dotty will study together."

Barker nodded. The twins jumped up and sat at the table by the window with Lavinia.

Russell yelled, "Come on back here, T.T." T.T. asked the boy who sat behind me to study with him and Russell. Not even his buddies wanted to bother with Bird when it came time to study. No one picked him, and no one picked me either.

I didn't mind because I knew all the work and didn't need anyone to study with anyhow. Bird took his textbook out of the desk and turned the pages slowly. There wasn't a smile anywhere near Bird's face. I thought about Amir again and what he'd do if he were in the class right now.

I raised my hand. "I'll study with Bird," I said. Seemed like the whole class stared at me. Bird looked shocked, and even Mrs. Barker was surprised. A girl in the front of the room said, "Miss Smartness and Yellow Bird?"

Barker hushed her. Then she turned to Bird. "This time is for studying, James, not playing."

Bird still looked shocked when he sat down near me at Mickey's empty desk. "Why you pick me?" he whispered.

"Because I wanted to."

Bird looked at me like he didn't believe I meant it. "Really?" he said.

I nodded.

He looked over at Barker, who was at her desk doing paperwork. "If you just explain the main things, I'll remember and write the dates down," he said. "But I mix up the numbers sometimes."

I opened my book. "Let's read this part here. It's important."

"Can you just explain it to me? Or . . . or . . . read it to me? See, sometimes I can read the words. But it takes so long to figure them out, I forget what I read in the beginning by the time I get to the end."

"You probably forget when you fool around." I looked at him cautiously. "But you serious now, right?"

He nodded. "I always have been, Doris. But I get confused. Most times I think which words make sense and just guess. Sometimes all the words look backwards."

"How did you know all the answers to the questions, like when we studied King Tut?"

"I remembered everything you read to me. And it was interesting. Sometimes I can read long words better than short ones because I remember how the long ones look. Like I can read the word *electricity*," he said proudly.

Barker looked over at us. "Come on, Bird," I said, "Let's read before she starts fussing."

I read to him quietly while he followed along in his book. He copied the important dates on a piece of paper. I wrote a word or name to go with them. He memorized the names. It took a long time to go through that, but he was happy when we finished.

"I think I know it now, Doris. Thank you."

"Okay, Bird. Let's go over the dates again to make sure you still remember them." I noticed Lavinia and the twins peeping at us. Let them wonder, I said to myself.


Bird didn't come to the cafeteria at lunchtime. I didn't see him again until the afternoon class. I expected that any minute he'd be his old self again—throw a wad of paper at T.T. or make a funny noise during the science film. He was quiet all afternoon. A new Bird, maybe . . .

At three o'clock, he stood next to me when we lined up for dismissal. "Doris, can I study with you this afternoon?" He stared at the floor.

I couldn't believe this new shy person standing in front of me.

"But we already studied for the test."

"Doris, I mean, like, can we do homework together?"

I searched his face for a grin on his lips or a smile in his eyes. He was dead serious. "Okay, Bird. But you gotta come to my house."

We left the room and walked down the stairs. "Your mother won't mind?" he said.

"Not unless she needs me to mind Gerald."

When we were outside of the school, T.T. pulled Bird by his arm.

"Come on the playground, man."

Bird shook his head. "I got to study."

"Study what?" T.T. looked puzzled.

I sucked my teeth. "You never heard of doing homework?"

T.T. grinned at us. "Now this a strange combination. Doris and Yellow Bird?" He hooted like an owl and ran across the street to the playground.

I didn't care what T.T. thought. He could tell the whole school if he wanted to. Yellow Bird was a good person and maybe he was even my friend. And besides, since I decided to help Yellow Bird, I was starting to feel like Amir was back again, right here on 163rd Street.

# 9

## A NEW OLD FRIEND

A NEW OLD FRIEND

"Hi, Ma," I yelled as we entered the living room.

Bird seemed a little nervous. He knew how strict my mother is.

"Mrs. Williams?" he asked as politely as he could. "Can Doris help me with my homework this afternoon?"

Ma walked into the room with Gerald toddling behind her. Gerald scrambled into my father's big, raggedy leather chair and jumped up and down grinning at Bird. Ma picked him up and put him back on the floor. "Doris has her own homework to do."

"But Mrs. Williams, Doris is the best student in class. No one can help me like her." Bird made his face sweet as sugar.

"Sometimes Doris can't help her own self." Ma smiled. "Go on in the kitchen, but you can't stay too long."

Bird knew just what to say to Ma. She took it very personal whenever I got a compliment. "How's your mother?" Ma asked as Bird followed her into the kitchen. "Haven't seen her in a while."

"She's okay," he said quickly. He spread his books out on the table and I sat across from him.

When Ma took Gerald inside for his nap, I whispered to Bird. "You in a lot of trouble with your father?"

"No. He just said I better not mess up again." Bird tried to look like everything was okay, but his eyes were scared.

"What your mother say?"

"Nothing." I could tell he didn't want to talk about her.

We had to write one of Barker's one-page compositions for homework. The theme was future plans. I pushed a sheet of paper in front of him. "Guess we better get the composition out the way first," I said.

"Doris, I can't do it."

"Barker will know if I do it for you."

"Let me say it and then you write what I say. Only print so I can read it when I copy it in my own writing."

"You can't read script?"

He shook his head. "Takes me a long time to figure out what the words are. Sometimes it seem like the letters run together."

"Maybe you need glasses," I said.

He shook his head. "No, it ain't like that. My eyes are fine. There's just something wrong with me. I see words sort of backwards. Like this word here." He pointed to the word *was*. "Sometime I read it as *saw*."

I stared at my notebook. "I used to do that when I was little and just learning how to read."

He avoided my eyes. "But you don't do it anymore.

It ain't normal for someone old as me to still be doing that."

"I saw a television show once about a girl who had trouble reading, but she was very smart."

"That's not like me; I ain't so smart." He hit himself in the head and stuck his tongue out at the same time. "See, something's wrong."

He looked so silly I couldn't help laughing.

"You play too much — that's why you have trouble in school," I said. "Come on, Bird, composition time."

He dictated to me and I wrote. "My future plans are, I want to sing and dance and act and have a good time in life."

"Bird, you know that's going to make Barker mad. You supposed to say something serious."

He stared at me with his round eyes, and I expected any minute for him to cross his eyes or make a funny face, but he wasn't joking.

"I am serious. Actors, and singers, and dancers. Ain't they serious about what they do?"

"You better take out having a good time, then," I said.

"Why?"

"Because it ain't serious if you enjoy it. You gotta say something like 'I want to be a doctor so I can cure diseases. Help sick people' — something necessary."

"Actors, singers, and dancers ain't necessary?"

"If someone is laying down sick as a dog, who you think they gonna call, Bird? A doctor or a singer?"

"Well, the singer or actor make you forget how bad

you feel. The doctor remind you how sick you is."

"Bird, you just saying this to get on Barker's last nerve."

"No." He twisted around in the chair. "I mean what I say. That's what I want to be. Nothing else. Anyway, I hate everything else. Especially anything where I have to read or write. 'Cause I can't do them so good."

"You can do it when you concentrate," I said. "Now, Bird, say something that ain't gonna send Barker to ape city."

Bird dictated again: "I want to be an actor, and a dancer, and a singer because I'm good at all of them. When you're an actor, you can be different people — not just one boring person. And you can make people happy. Make them forget their problems — Is it good so far, Doris?"

"Yeah, yeah," I said. "Just don't say nothing about having fun."

He picked up his pen and began to copy what I'd written for him.

He stared at me, but it was like he was seeing something else. "My mother took me to see a play on Broadway when I was little. It was the first time I saw real people on a stage — not like television. Mama said, 'They're real people, like you and me.' "

He continued copying while I started my homework. It was strange being in my kitchen, studying quietly with Bird. We heard my mother in the living room singing to Gerald all out of tune. Bird looked up from his paper. "My mother is gone," he said.

"Gone? Where?"

"Went to Virginia. My grandmother is sick. She has to take care of her."

"That's too bad. She's gonna be there a long time?"

He shrugged his shoulders. "I don't know. I miss her. Just me and my old man in the house."

I guess it was hard on Bird to be there alone with his mean-looking father. His mother was a nice, quiet lady. I used to wonder how she could have a wild child like Bird.

We went over the reading assignment. I had to tell him almost every other word, but he tried hard. I remembered how patient Amir was when he helped Bird. Giving him a chance to figure out the words himself. Then not making Bird feel bad when he had to end up telling him the word. Some people make you feel very stupid when you make a mistake. I treated Bird the same way Amir would've treated him.

After I practically read the whole story to Bird, he could recite it back to me like he'd read it by himself a hundred times. Ma came into the kitchen just as Bird finished. "How're the scholars doing?" she said, looking at Bird. "I didn't know you was so serious. And Doris, I didn't know you was such a fine little teacher."

She put on her apron. "You-all almost finished?"

Bird stood up before I answered. "We finished, Mrs. Williams."

"I'm not rushing you," Ma said smiling.

She seemed to like him, which surprised me. Ma could be so fussy sometimes — especially about my friends, but she liked Amir also.

I walked Bird to the door.

"Thanks, Doris." He looked down at his shoes. Here comes the shy person again, I thought.

"Doris, you know, you real nice. That's what I keep telling people."

"What people?"

He looked up at the peeling paint on the ceiling. "You know, people in the class. When they say you hinkty and stuck-up."

"I ain't thinking about them people in the class. Especially you-know-who."

He looked down at his feet again. "I'm going to do better in class so I can join the Drama Club. Why don't you join too?"

I shook my head. "No way."

He shifted his weight from one foot to the other. "Maybe you'll change your mind, huh, Doris?"

"I doubt it. I'll see you tomorrow, Bird."

I went back to the kitchen to finish my homework. Bird left a piece of paper that he'd started to write on crumpled up on the table. I picked it up and read it. He had a nice way of printing, but when he copied he left out words and forgot to cross his *t*'s.

Bird was funny. Sometimes he seem so silly and immature. But when he got serious, he was a whole different person. Sometimes he'd say things that were so intelligent I'd wonder if there was really a regular person inside of him. Amir would be pleased with me if I could keep Bird serious long enough to get him into the Drama Club and pass his studies for the year. But you never knew with Bird.

## 10

I pulled my coat tight as I walked to school. It'd soon be time for heavy winter boots. I passed the Beauty Hive as I crossed the street to the playground so I could take the shortcut to school. I had to go to the Beauty Hive again on Saturday to tell Miss Bee I couldn't work. I had more time to earn money to visit Amir since he wasn't ready to see me. By the time he was ready, I would be able to convince Ma to let me work at the Hive and go to visit Amir.

When I got to the library, I was surprised to see Bird waiting for me at the table by the window. The only person missing now was Amir. Even though helping Bird almost brought Amir back — the way we used to help him together.

"Hi, Doris," he whispered loudly.

"Hello, Bird," I said, putting my books on the table.

He opened his math workbook. "Doris, will you help me with these fractions?"

While we went over the fractions, I expected him to suddenly be the old Bird, but he never even looked around. It was funny. While I helped Bird I began to feel as if I was doing something important and grown-up — the same way I felt the first time I worked at Miss Bee's.

"Bird, you're doing the steps correctly, but you keep getting the wrong answer," I said. He frowned and started erasing.

"Oh, I see what it is," I said. "It's like you said. You're twisting them numbers around." I pointed to his paper. "That should be twelve, not twenty-one. You're doing the problems right and you're getting the right answers. You're just getting mixed up when you write them down."

Bird grinned like I really understood him. As soon as we finished, the bell rang.

Bird was on his best behavior in class. He didn't ask for a pass to the bathroom or play around with T.T. Barker made us go over the English homework. We had to discuss and read out loud in class the same story we read for homework.

Bird buried his head in his book, like an ostrich burying its head in sand. He could read a few of the words, and he probably remembered all of the story, but I knew he was praying Barker wouldn't call on him.

Fortunately for Bird, Barker didn't bother him. When we came to the end of the story, there was a short paragraph left to read. Some students volunteered, and Bird raised his hand a little as if he wasn't sure that he really wanted to try.

I looked over the paragraph quickly. The words weren't too hard, but Bird might still have trouble. He raised his hand higher. Barker glanced at him and called on a girl in the first row. She wouldn't even give him a chance to try. Bird put his hand down and didn't raise it again for the rest of the day.

Barker acted like he wasn't in the room. She didn't even fuss when he tried to write a composition and never finished. She didn't collect his paper either. I wondered what she had up her sleeve.

Bird came home with me again that afternoon. He didn't even ask, but just walked with me to 163rd Street and kept walking with me as I climbed the stairs to my apartment. "Don't you have to let your father know you home from school?" I asked.

Bird looked at me like I was crazy. "No. My father works nights and he glad I ain't there disturbing him while he sleeping in the afternoon."

I guess no one else has to deal with the old-fashioned rules my parents think up.

The delicious smell of a roasting chicken greeted us when we walked in the house. Gerald almost fell on his face running toward Bird. I wondered what Ma would say about Bird coming over again.

He sat at the kitchen table and immediately took out his books. Guess he didn't want my mother to misunderstand why he was there.

Ma pushed the bowl filled with apples and oranges toward him. I relaxed.

"No thank you, Mrs. Williams."

"Boy, go on and take a piece of fruit. You-all come home from school hungry."

"He don't like fruit," I said.

She patted Gerald's head as he clung to her leg. "Fruit's good for you."

Bird took a loud bite out of an apple. He'd do anything to stay on my mother's good side. Even eat fruit. Ma left the kitchen, and we began our homework.

"Let's go over the dates for the social studies test tomorrow," he said, flipping the pages of his book.

"We better get the homework done first. You already know those dates."

"I never do good on tests. Especially if I have to remember dates."

"You'll do fine, Bird. You worry too much about them dates."

I looked through my notebook for the English homework.

Bird looked down at the table. "I know people be laughing at me when I can't read and stuff," he said out of the clear blue sky.

I sucked my teeth. "They just stupid. Always laughing at somebody. You wasn't trying before and concentrating like you are now. I bet you start reading better." I didn't think that Bird worried about people laughing at him.

After we finished the English homework, Bird insisted that we practice the dates again. He got them all correct.

"You know those dates like you know your name,"
I said.

Ma came in the kitchen. "Okay, Professor Doris,"
she said, "let's clear this table. Your father'll be home
soon."

She watched Bird when he stood up. "Boy, you still
wearing that piece of sweater in this cold?"

"I'm all right, Mrs. Williams."

She started to say something when Daddy put his
key in the door.

"Whatever is in them pots smells good," he called
from the living room. When he walked into the kitchen,
Gerald tripped on his own feet running to him. Daddy
picked him up and swung him in the air.

"Hello, son," he said to Bird. "How's your old man
and your mother? Ain't seen them in a long time."

"They okay," Bird said quietly and picked up his
books. "Good night everybody," he said. "See you tomorrow, Doris."

Ma gave him one of her mind-reading looks. "I
haven't seen your mother in a while. How is she?"

He stared at the floor. "Okay. She's . . . she's taking
care of my grandmother in Virginia."

Daddy lifted up the roasting pan. "Have dinner with
us," he said.

I could tell Bird wanted to say yes, but he buttoned
his sweater.

"No, sir, I'm not hungry."

Ma said, "Don't your father work nights?"

"Yes."

"You're in the house alone. Don't be shame. Eat

with us. One more mouth ain't gonna send us to the poorhouse," Ma said.

It was funny how Ma took to Bird. Daddy liked everyone, but Ma was harder to please.

Bird peeped at me shyly while we ate. He acted like a different person around my family. When we finished eating, he helped me clean the table and wash the dishes. He played with Gerald and acted like he didn't want to go home.

After Gerald had laughed himself silly at Bird's clown faces, Ma said, "Son, Doris will see you tomorrow. It's getting late."

"Okay, Mrs. Williams," Bird said as he put Gerald on the floor.

"What time does your father come home from work?" she asked him. I don't know why she was giving poor Bird the third degree.

"When I leave for school."

"He doesn't notice how you don't dress for the weather?"

"I'm not cold, ma'am."

As he walked out of the door, she yelled after him, "Better put on a heavier jacket tomorrow."

"Yes, ma'am," he called back.

Bird stood on my stoop when I came downstairs in the morning. Pretty soon he'd started meeting me every morning and coming home with me every afternoon. I was spending so much time studying with Bird, that I was really learning everything too.

When the day of the big social studies test rolled

around, he rattled off the dates for the test as we walked up the block, huddling close together for warmth against the wind.

Bird seemed happy and confident when we went to class. Mrs. Barker gave us time for last-minute study. Bird concentrated quietly. Russell volunteered to give out the test. He slowly squeezed his big self between the rows of desks.

Barker stood in front of the room. "Everything away. Close all books and put them under your seats. Do not pick up your pens until I tell you to. Mickey, spit out that gum." She stared at T.T. "Sit up straight, young man. Okay. Begin."

The test was about Egypt, and the room was quiet except for the sounds of pens scratching on paper. Barker sat at her desk marking our homework. Even though her head was down, I was sure she saw everything.

Suddenly, there was a big crash. She stood up so quickly that her chair fell over. "James Towers, what are you doing?"

Bird jumped up as Barker barreled toward him, red as a sunset. Bird got paler and the little patch of hair on top of his head looked like it was saluting.

"Give me that paper. I saw you!"

His mouth moved back and forth, but nothing came out.

"We don't cheat on tests in this class. I want the paper now." She snatched his arm and a piece of paper fell to the floor. She picked it up.

Bird stammered. "I . . . I . . . studied. It was the

dates. I mix up the numbers. I wr-wr-wrote the dates so I wouldn't mix up the numbers. They're just the dates. I didn't write down what they was for."

"Don't make excuses, young man. This is intolerable behavior."

I wanted to raise my hand and tell her that Bird knew the dates this morning. If only I could explain to her what was wrong with Bird and how hard he tried. That he wasn't really a cheat, even though he had a paper with the dates on them. Why couldn't she see that there was something smart and good in Bird? The way Amir taught me to see. I wanted to tell her all those things.

"Sit in the back, young man. You'll be taken care of later."

Bird walked slowly to the back of the room and sat down. I continued working on the test, but I couldn't concentrate. I had to speak. Barker never gave Bird a chance to show what he could do. My hand shook a little as I raised it. "Mrs. Barker?"

She was still in a red rage. "Yes."

"Mrs. Barker, you don't understand Bird," I said. "He wasn't cheating."

Mrs. Barker glared at me. "Young lady, I don't need *you* to tell me what I don't understand. Let's not forget which of us is the teacher."

Someone giggled as I slid down in my seat as far as I could. My face got hot. I felt like a fool.

I lowered my head and tried to continue, and noticed Mickey staring at me. If Barker only knew how hard Bird had studied.

I turned around and quickly glanced at Bird, who covered his face with his hands. All I could see was the top of his head. I felt like putting my arms around his shoulders — the way I do with Gerald when he's upset. The feeling surprised me.

Suddenly Bird left his seat and ran out of the room, slamming the door in Barker's surprised face. I closed my eyes and shook my head — Bird did it again.

# 11
## A LITTLE
## HELP
## FROM MY
## FRIEND

Instead of eating at lunchtime, I looked for Bird in the schoolyard and the playground but he wasn't there. I ran back to school and went to the library, but he wasn't there, either. I looked in the gym before the bell rang for afternoon classes. He was nowhere around.

Why did he do it? He knew the dates, and he know Barker sees everything. Bird didn't return to class. I was so worried about Bird and angry at Barker, I couldn't think about anything else for the rest of the afternoon.

When I got home from school and walked in the kitchen, the first thing Ma said was, "Where's your friend? No studying this afternoon?"

I couldn't tell her what happened. She'd think Bird was wrong and she wouldn't let me see him anymore. I took an apple out of the fruit bowl. "Ma, can I go out and play before it's dark?"

"Oh, you made up with your friends?"

"I just want to go out for a while."

"What about your homework?"

"If I start it now, it'll be dark when I finish."

"Be back in here by five. And don't leave the block."

I ran to Bird's building, rang his bell, and hoped his father didn't answer. Finally, Bird came to the door. He opened it slightly and was surprised to see me. "Wait, Doris, I'll come outside."

I waited for him on his stoop. He sat down next to me as we silently watched two dogs chasing each other in the lot across the street. Bird picked up a stick and scraped it against the stoop.

"Why did you do it?" I asked. "After all that time we spent studying?"

He wouldn't look at me. "I wasn't cheating. I didn't want to mix up the dates."

"Why did you leave the room? Suppose you get suspended again?"

"I was mad. I left school for good. I'm never going to make it into the Drama Club, and I'm never going to make it out of the sixth grade."

"Why didn't you try to explain to Barker? Tell her you was afraid of reversing the numbers?"

He looked at me. "You know you can't say nothing to Barker."

"You could've just tried to tell her you wasn't cheating."

He turned away from me again. "You don't understand, Doris. I mean, like I know the dates, but my mind, it's like my mind gets a cramp, I swear . . . and then I can't find the answer even though I know it."

"You mean you forget?"

"I don't know. Not really. It's right there" — he

banged his forehead — "but I can't get it out."

I stood up. "Bird, when things go wrong, you can't keep acting the fool and doing crazy things. It just makes Barker madder. You just got to ignore her when she act like that."

He got up slowly. "I know, but I can't. I get too mad."

Bird really needed a friend now, and I was glad to be his friend. "You want to have dinner with us tonight?" I knew my mother's cooking would make him feel better.

He nodded.

"Get your books, then, and I'll help you do your homework."

I had to do most of his work for him. He couldn't get anything straight in his head. Except those dates. We went over them again and he didn't confuse the numbers.

"You didn't need that paper. Why don't you explain to Barker and ask her to let you take the test again?"

"She hates me."

I scratched my head. Barker seemed to kind of like me a little bit sometimes. "I'll go with you. See, we'll just explain to her in a nice way when we go back to school on Monday."

Bird looked doubtful. "You better do most of the talking. She don't want to hear nothing I have to say."

"All you gotta do is apologize for leaving the room. Then we'll make her understand that you wasn't cheating."

When Bird left, I went back to the kitchen and put

the dried dishes in the cabinet. I figured that on Monday everything would be okay. We'd talk to Barker and explain the situation to her.

On Saturday afternoon, I ran into Bird on my way out of my building. I was going to try to quit my job again, if I could get up the nerve.

"Hey, Doris, I was wondering what you was doing today."

"Hi, Bird."

"Where you going?" He leaned on the railing leading to the basement.

"Listen, Bird, this just between you and me. I got this job at the Hive, but I have to quit. Do you mind looking out for my parents for me while I go in and quit?"

"Why you need money so bad?" he asked. "I know everybody on 163rd Street need money, but it ain't like your family starving."

"I wanted to go visit Amir, and train fare is fifty dollars. But he ain't ready to see anyone yet, so I got some time to make the money. And besides, my parents won't let me work."

"How are you going to make money if you're not allowed to work?" he asked me.

I shrugged.

"Do you really want to visit Amir?"

"More than anything."

He grabbed my wrists. "Hey, I got an idea. I can help you keep your job," he said.

"Get outta here, Bird," I said. "I can't keep my job.

My parents will put me under punishment until I'm thirty-five years old."

"You can," he said excitedly. "You ain't doing anything dangerous or bad. What if you just do a little bit more and then stop when you get fifty dollars?"

"I don't know, Bird."

"You got to let me do something for you, since you've been so nice to me. Let me just do this one thing for you. Listen, I'll be the lookout for you while you work." He talked on the side of his mouth like in one of them old-time gangster movies.

"No, Bird. I can't do it. I'll get into trouble. They really mean it."

"Come on, Doris. Let me save your life again."

I laughed. "I can see it now. My mother will run into Miss Bee on the street and Miss Bee say, 'Oh Honey Bunch is doing a wonderful job in my establishment,' " I said imitating her.

"Just tell Miss Bee you don't want your mother to know you working there because you're planning a big surprise for your mother."

"And if she knows I'm working, it won't be a surprise," I continued.

"Yeah." He nodded frantically. "Come on, Doris. Let me give you a hand."

"Maybe," I said. Bird was so intent on helping me, I was afraid I'd hurt him if I didn't say yes. We started walking toward the Hive.

"You'll have no problem with my help," he said, chuckling.

"Remember your help with the poem?" I said.

"Yeah, but I handled that paper-towel job like a pro."
He flexed his muscles and grinned. Then he stood still
in the middle of the block. "We need a system," he
said. "If your mother is coming, I'll hold up one finger. If the coast is clear, I'll hold up four fingers."

We started walking again. "I told Ma I was going to
the movies. I feel bad lying to her."

"You wasn't lying to her. You was going to the movies when you left. Now you're going to work."

"I guess so."

"Just remember, if I see your mother coming, it's
one finger. If I see your father coming, I'll hold up two
fingers."

"Dog, Bird, that's a lot to remember."

He shook his head. "No, Doris. It goes like this:
One for your mother, two for Dad, four for the folk
who think they bad."

I hit him on his back. "You so silly."

"We forgot Nosey Nicols," I said. "Look, one for
Ma, two for Pa, and three for Nosey; four, all clear.
See?" I giggled. "I got it now." I looked to the left
and right before I ducked into the Hive.

The cloud of smoke wasn't over Miss Bee's booth,
so I knew business was slow again this Saturday. Miss
Bee sat in her booth reading the paper. "Hi, Honey
Bunch," she said. "Nothing much happening today.
Got a lady coming in here at two."

The telephone rang, and my heart missed a beat.
"Set up the counter for me, Honey Bunch." She answered the phone.

I took the shampoos, lotions, and combs out of the cabinet. I wished some more little girls would come in to have their hair cornrowed. When Miss Bee finished her call, I told her how I wanted to keep my job a secret from my mother.

"Honey Bunch, you're a darling child. Your secret's good with me." She praised me so much I felt ashamed about lying.

I looked around for something else to do. Carol's and the other hairdresser's booths were clean. "Miss Bee, you want me to fold some towels?"

"Yes, sugar, and water the plant."

I sighed. Her and that plant. "You sure it ain't dead?"

"No, it's got some life in it still. You wait till spring."

I stretched my hand as far as I could and tried to hide behind the curtain and reach for the plant. It didn't look any better to me than it did last week. I took it to the back and watered it.

The telephone rang, and my heart thumped again as Miss Bee answered it. It wasn't my mother. She'd probably never call again unless someone told her they saw me in here.

When I went back to the window, Bird was standing outside holding up ten fingers and grinning. He couldn't help acting crazy.

I waved him away and then he held up four fingers — the all-clear sign. He ran up the block. Bird was a perfect lookout, but there was nothing to watch out for.

I started feeling guilty after about an hour, so I told

Miss Bee that I had to go home and help my mother.

"Honey Bunch, no point in hanging around here," Miss Bee said after I folded the towels. "Things won't get jumping until the holidays." She reached down in her pocket, "Here's a little tip for coming and pulling out them supplies and watering my plant." She handed me $1.00.

I looked up and down the block before I stepped out of the Hive. It was a relief to get out of there. Bird was near my building throwing a basketball between the rungs of the fire escape, looking proud of himself.

"Hey, Doris." He held up four fingers.

The sun shining right on the stoop took the chill off. The air was crisp and fresh. I sat down.

"You finished already?" he asked, resting his basketball on the stoop.

"Yeah, and thanks a lot. I finished early." I didn't tell him why. "Want to go to the Plaza and see a movie?"

"*Blazing Guns* and *Monster of the Dead and Dying* is still there," Bird said. "I saw them both last week." He grabbed his skinny hips like a cowboy grabbing a holster. I leaned back on the stoop and watched as Bird acted out the whole movie.

"Now let me tell you about *Monster of the Dead*. You got some tissues?"

I dug down in my pocket and found half a package of Kleenex. Bird took the tissues out of the packet and stuffed them in his mouth. He looked like a frog and roared like a lion.

Mrs. Nicols walked down the steps, looked at Bird

and shook her head. I didn't even want to speak to her, but I had to. Otherwise she'd run me in to my mother, complaining that I was rude. "Hi, Mrs. Nicols," I said. "How are you today?"

Bird said, "Hi, Mrs. Nicols, ma'am," and then he lowered his arms and growled some more.

Mrs. Nicols adjusted her flowered hat. "I love to see happy children," she said and tipped on down the street. A man passing by grinned at Bird's antics too.

When Bird finished, he sat next to me on the stoop. Then he tried to spin his basketball on his index finger. Suddenly, he looked very serious. "Wonder what Barker will say to me on Monday?"

"Don't worry about her. We'll explain everything." I put my hand on his shoulder. "Anyway, thanks, Bird."

"For what?"

"For being my lookout."

"As long as you have me watching, you can keep your job."

I hugged my knees tightly against my chest as Bird grinned happily to himself. But what was I really going to do about my job at the Hive?

# 12
## A NEW
## VENTURE

12
A NEW
VENTURE

Bird wasn't waiting for me on my stoop when I got downstairs the next morning, but I didn't think anything was wrong. I figured he'd be in the library. He wasn't there, and he wasn't on line in the cafeteria.

Every time the classroom door opened I thought Bird would walk in. But he never did.

Russell and T.T. asked me about Bird at lunchtime. "I hope he wasn't suspended," Russell said.

I stared at the cold macaroni on my plate, but I couldn't eat. "There are kids who've done worse things than Bird and they wasn't suspended."

"Barker really has it in for him," T.T. said.

I thought about Bird all afternoon. I couldn't think about anything else. Barker had to be set straight about Bird, and I was going to do it.

When everyone left at three o'clock, I thought of a million reasons to go home and not talk to her, but I knew I had to.

I lingered around in the classroom, then I took a deep breath and walked up to her desk. "Mrs. Barker

. . . I . . ." My voice came out in a babyish whine.

She gave me a stern look. "Yes, Doris?"

I breathed deeply again. "What is going to happen to Bird?" I blurted out quickly.

"That's no business of yours." She was reddening up.

I don't know where I got the nerve from. "Mrs. Barker. Bird wasn't cheating. He ain't a bad person."

"*Isn't* a bad person," she said slowly. "Now you listen to me, young lady!" She wagged her finger in my face. "You need to stay away from kids like James. You're a bright girl. People like James will bring you down."

"Mrs. Barker. Bird studied for that test. I know, because I helped him. He gets the numbers mixed up; that's why he had the paper," I said quickly before she interrupted me.

"You helped him?" she asked.

I nodded.

She looked vaguely interested. "You don't understand Bird," I said boldly.

Mrs. Barker stiffened. "I understand him very well. And if you continue to show me disrespect by telling me how to run my affairs, I will have to inform your parents."

I wished I could red up like her so she could see how mad I was. I couldn't let her tell my parents. They might think Bird was wrong, and they wouldn't let me see him. I walked out the door and got away from Barker before I got into any more trouble.

I hadn't said anything that I wanted to say or the way I wanted to say it. Barker was probably running to the office now to call my mother and tell that I'd sassed her. I wondered if Ma would take up for me, or if she'd know that Barker had no reason to get me into trouble. I guess I got too mad. Amir would have known how to speak to Barker.

I took the shortcut through the playground to see whether Bird was there. Some little kids played on the swings, and Russell and the other guys were at the basketball court. Bird was nowhere in sight.

I decided to stop by his house. The lock was broken on the outside door, so I just walked right into his dark hallway. As I ran up the four flights of stairs to his apartment, I prayed his father wouldn't answer. I knocked lightly on the door, and when no one came, I knocked again.

"Who is it?" His father sounded like I'd woke him up.

"Is . . . is Bird, I mean, James there?" I said softly.

"He ain't home from school yet," he said gruffly.

"Thank you," I said, and tore down the stairs in case he opened the door.

I went home. Ma didn't say anything when I walked in, so I knew Barker hadn't called her. Maybe Bird would come over later and explain what was going on.

I didn't see or hear from Bird all evening.

The following morning, I looked around for Bird on the way to school. It was too cold to stay in the street if he was playing hooky. His father was home during the day, so I knew he wasn't hanging out there.

He wasn't in the library or in the cafeteria when we lined up for class. I hadn't really thought about Barker again until she came to take us upstairs. I wondered whether she'd say anything to me about our conversation yesterday. She didn't speak directly to me. She just made a remark to the whole class about picking and choosing friends wisely.

We had assembly later that morning. When we walked in the auditorium, I saw Mr. Lowe, the assistant principal, standing near a group of students from one of the special classes. Those kids were all squirming around and talking when everyone else was quiet. He yelled at a boy who popped in and out of his seat. I saw Bird slumped way down in the next seat. He wore a blue hooded sweatshirt pulled over his head like he wanted to hide his face. What was he doing with them? I wondered.

"Bird," I whispered loudly. Mrs. Barker put her finger to her lips and glared at me, and Bird sunk deeper into his seat.

When the assembly was over, Bird was gone. I thought he'd come over to us and go back upstairs with our class, but he didn't. I had to find out what had happened to him, so as soon as we got back, I asked Mrs. Barker for a pass to the bathroom.

I ran downstairs to the first floor where the special classes are. I looked for the one that I saw Bird with at assembly. A lot of yelling and screaming came out of a third room. I peeped inside. Bird was standing on top of a clothes closet, flapping his arms back and forth, threatening to fly. One girl, who couldn't talk well, said, "Fry, fry, the boy can fry."

Bird was in the class with the kids who used a toy clock to learn how to tell time and play money in order to learn how to make change. The two teachers in the room tried to get Bird to come down off the closet. Then I heard a familiar voice behind me.

"Young lady, are you enjoying the show?"

I turned around and could hardly speak. "Mr. Wash-Washington, I —"

"I think you'd better get to where you're going before —" He stopped when he saw Bird leap onto a chair. The girl yelled, "He fry! The boy can fry!" Mr. Washington ran in the room.

"Get out of here and leave this class alone," he shouted at Bird. "For someone who wants to get into the Drama Club, you're certainly taking the wrong approach."

The teacher looked like she was going to cry. "He's assigned to this class," she said. Mr. Washington was shocked, and I know I looked like I had been electrocuted too.

Mr. Washington said to the teacher, "Let me talk to him for a minute."

"Keep him as long as you like," she said.

Bird kept his face down as he came out into the hall and closed the door behind him. He still had his hood on.

"Take that hood off your head and look at me," Mr. Washington said.

Bird lifted his head and tried to face Mr. Washington. His eyes looked at the wall, the ceiling, everywhere except at Mr. Washington.

"Man, what's wrong with you? Why are you making a spectacle of yourself, disrespecting the teacher, upsetting the whole class. When I saw you the other day, I was excited to have such an enthusiastic and bright student in the club. But, boy, you act like this, and we count you out!"

Bird dropped his head again and didn't answer.

"Mr. Washington," I said, "Bird ain't like them other kids."

"No. The other kids were sitting in their seats acting like they know what to do in a classroom."

"But, Mr. Washington, Bird is smart."

"I know what you mean." He turned to Bird again. "Mrs. Barker said you were a problem." He lifted Bird's chin and made him look in his face. "You see where your behavior got you?"

Bird didn't say a word.

"Mr. Washington," I said, "Bird is a serious actor and he wants to join the club, but Mrs. Barker says he can't."

"She's not his teacher now," Mr. Washington said. "I'll take him in the club. But man, you better not act the fool with me. You hear?"

"Yes," Bird said quietly.

"And you're going to get your act together in this class too?"

"Yes."

"If you don't, no club and no chance to be in the show."

"I thought I couldn't be in it because of my grades and because I was put out of my regular class," Bird said hesitantly.

Mr. Washington looked closely at Bird. "Teachers can recommend students to me, but if I see a student who has potential or talent, then I can take him in the program. And I think you might have some talent." Mr. Washington glanced over at me.

"The play and the club are for everyone who wants to be in them." The vein in Mr. Washington's temple moved back and forth. "Get back in that class, and behave yourself. I'm going to be checking on you."

Bird went in the room and Mr. Washington followed him. I waited outside in the hallway for Mr. Washington to come out. I couldn't understand how Bird could've been put in that class. I sat down on the staircase next to Bird's room and covered my face and cried. I felt bad for Bird. Barker, the principal, and whoever else had taken him out of our class were wrong. How could they put him in a class where some of the kids could hardly speak? Bird belonged with us, in room 402.

When Mr. Washington came out, he handed me a tissue, and I wiped my eyes and blew my nose. He sat down next to me on the steps. "Mr. Washington," I said. "Bird ain't like them other kids. I've been helping him with his homework, and he's got just a little something wrong with him."

Mr. Washington looked kind. He didn't correct my

grammar or get mad at me for not minding my business. "How so, Doris?" he said.

I explained to him how Bird was seeing things mixed up and he had trouble reading, and Mr. Washington said he'd look into it more and make sure that Bird got the help he needed. And he thanked me for being so caring. I didn't think I was being caring, though. I just wanted to help my friend.

I didn't say anything to anyone about where Bird was. I didn't even tell his buddies — Russell and T.T. When we were dismissed at three, I rushed outside. I waited for Bird, but he never came down the school steps. He must've left early or come out of one of the side exits.

Then I remembered that the students in the special classes left a little earlier. That's why no one saw him. Instead of walking down Cauldwell Avenue to 163rd Street, I took the shortcut through the playground.

When I got to the 163rd Street exit, I saw him. "Bird," I yelled. "Wait up."

For a minute it looked like he was going to run from me, but he stopped. I caught up to him. "Why didn't you tell me?"

He wouldn't look at me. "I couldn't."

"You're not like those kids. I don't mean to talk bad about them or anything like that, but you're not like them."

"Yes, I am. I can't read," he said in a choked-up voice. He sounded like he was going to cry and I felt like crying again.

"You read a little. I mean, all you have to do is keep being serious like you been."

He turned his back to me and shook his head.

I didn't know what to say to him. "You're in the club now and that should be fun, Bird." I touched the arm of his jacket. He didn't move.

I expected him to turn around smiling that old Yellow Bird smile. Instead he shrugged his shoulders.

"You ain't interested in it anymore?" I asked.

"How can I be in a play if I can't read the script? How can I be an actor?"

We started walking toward the block. "You used to do the same work we did, Bird. I'll help you read the script. That ain't no big thing. And you know maybe we can get Mr. Washington to talk to Barker if you do real good in the play. Maybe she'll let you back in the class."

Bird was silent.

"Maybe this class change is only for a little while. They just trying to scare you, Bird. I bet they let you back in our class."

Bird stared at me and shook his head again. We reached my building. "You want to do homework with me?" I asked.

"For what? I can do the work in my new class. One plus one equals two and *t-h-e* spells *the*." He shivered a little and rubbed his hands together. "And we don't get homework."

He sunk back in his hood, and I started climbing the steps.

"Study with me anyway," I said, looking back at him. "That way you'll know the work when you get back in our class."

He followed me up the stairs. "I'll never get back," he mumbled. "And I didn't know the work when I was in the class."

"That ain't true. You knew all the social studies. And you knew them dates, too."

When we sat down at the kitchen table, Bird turned the pages of my social studies book slowly. "Something's wrong with my head," he whispered.

There was nothing I could say. We just sat there quietly for a while listening to my mother talking to Gerald in the next room. Then I said, "Bird, I'm going to read Amir's letter to you." I went in my room and came back with the letter. "I wasn't going to show this to anyone, but I'll show it to you." Bird grinned at me like he was pleased.

"I still miss that dude sometimes," he said sadly, his face kind of clouding up.

I miss him all the time, I thought to myself. "It's too bad he had to leave," I said.

"But he's happy. And he better off where he is than he was with that foster family here in the Bronx. We should be happy something good happened for him."

Bird's mood changed slowly. We talked on and on about what a good time we all had together when Amir was living on 163rd Street. I loved to talk about him with Bird. Amir seemed more real and closer to me than ever.

"Hey, Doris," Bird said, suddenly excited. "Why don't you join the Drama Club too?"

I shook my head. "No. Not me. I don't want to be in no club, especially with them troublemaking girls."

"You'd be there with me. Me and you, Doris."

"I told you, I'd help you read a script, but I ain't joining."

"If you don't join, I ain't either," he said.

"You promised Mr. Washington."

His happy mood was disappearing, and he was beginning to look the same sad way he did when I saw him at three o'clock. "Doris, I don't want to to be in it if you don't come too."

"That's silly," I said. "You like to dance and act, not me."

"I don't want to go there alone," he muttered.

"Alone? You know everyone in the club."

His eyes looked pained. "Russell, Lavinia, and them, you know, they'll be laughing at me about being in that special class."

"They laugh at everyone, Bird. I just showed you the nice things Amir said about you."

"Amir ain't here, and you're my best friend, right?"

I didn't know what to say. At first I'd helped Bird because that's what Amir would've done. But lately I looked for Bird and worried about Bird because *I* really cared about what happened to him.

"I'll go with you to the meeting, but I ain't joining," I said.

"Join," he said. "Please?"

If I was going to help Bird, I thought, I'd have to go anyway. "Maybe I will," I said. "Yeah, maybe I will."

He jumped out of the chair and almost knocked me out of my seat when he ran over to me and gave me a big kiss on my cheek.

"You so crazy, Bird," I chuckled, rubbing my face, and I was glad he was my friend.

I felt real excited when me and Bird entered the auditorium. Practically the whole class was there along with kids from other classes, and two other teachers. Mr. Washington sat on the stage talking excitedly while his legs and sneakered feet dangled over the edge.

T.T. sat in the first row along with Lavinia, Russell, and Mickey and Dotty.

"I thought T.T. didn't want to be in the club," I said to Bird.

He frowned. "Guess he changed his mind, and Barker let him join."

"I bet if you're good in this play, Barker will let you come back in the class," I said as we sat down in the back of the auditorium.

Bird pulled the seat down so hard that Mr. Washington heard him.

"Come on up front," he said to us. It seemed like every head in the room turned around, and every eye was on Bird and me.

Lavinia put her hands over her mouth and whispered to Mickey.

"Hey, Bird!" Russell yelled when he saw us. "Where you been hiding?" His face split into a big grin. Russell knew.

Mr. Washington stood up and looked at Russell. "This ain't homecoming. You socialize after the meeting," he said.

Russell faced front, but T.T. still stared at us with a smile the size of a half-moon. "Ignore them, Bird," I whispered. "You better off without friends anyway."

He slumped down in the seat and stared at his hands. I nudged him. "Bird, you'll do so good in the play that nobody will tease you about being in that class."

Mr. Washington swung himself down from the stage and leaned against it. "Mrs. Barker tells me you are reading *A Christmas Carol* by Charles Dickens in your English studies. Who can tell me what it's about?"

"I can," T.T. called out. "It's that cool story about that Scrooge dude. He's rich, but he's real stingy. I saw a cartoon about him on television."

"Very good, T.T.," Mr. Washington said. "I was thinking of us updating that story."

Lavinia giggled. "T.T. could be the ghost of Christmas past."

Bird looked up slowly and whispered to me, "You really think I'd be good in a play?"

I nodded.

Bird grinned.

"We're going to do an adaptation. We'll have a Scrooge-type character, but we won't call him Scrooge," Mr. Washington said.

Lavinia raised her hand. "He could be a mean old man."

"Or a mean young woman," I said to myself.

"Right," Mr. Washington said, "how do we show his meanness?"

"He beats people up," a boy hollered.

Mr. Washington looked concerned. "I don't think we want to be violent, although that's a very good illustration of meanness."

"He's cheap," Bird whispered, "like the real Scrooge."

"Give your idea too, Bird," I said.

"Naw," he shook his head, "you say it for me."

"It's your idea, Bird." I pulled his arm up.

Mr. Washington nodded in our direction. "James?"

"What if . . . what if . . . ?" Bird stuttered. Someone snickered.

"The man is cheap," I finished. Then I raised my hand. "That was Bird's idea," I said.

Mickey giggled.

"It's a good idea," Mr. Washington said. "We can show the meanness in his character through his cheapness." Mr. Washington put his hands in his pockets and paced back and forth quickly. "Okay, now I want you to think of some characters and scenes." He stopped pacing and took a pad and pencil out of his briefcase. "I'll jot down your thoughts."

Bird raised his hand by himself this time. "He could have a lot of money but won't share it with nobody — not even his own family."

Mickey said, "Yeah, and he don't even help no one in any kind of way."

"These are wonderful suggestions," Mr. Washington said, writing quickly.

Bird pulled off his hood. Dotty waved her hands excitedly and stood up. "The man owns a building. Charges people too much rent and throws them out in the cold dark night if they can't pay." She hugged herself and shivered.

Mickey pulled her back in her seat. "Why don't you stop acting stupid?"

"And the man could hate Christmas the most out of all the holidays," I whispered to Bird.

Bird raised his hand.

"Yes, James." Mr. Washington continued to write while he listened.

"Doris has an idea. Suppose the man hates Christmas the most of all the holidays?"

Lavinia snickered and said something to Mickey again.

Mr. Washington looked up from his pad and smiled at us. "You and Doris speak for each other, right?" He wrote my idea on the board.

I was proud that he used my idea, even though I was embarrassed when somebody giggled.

"That was a great idea, Doris. We can call the play *The Man Who Hated Christmas*." He wrote real fast.

Everybody contributed ideas — even the two teachers. Then Mr. Washington talked to us about creating characters and writing and acting out scenes. Time flew and even though I didn't mean to, I started getting interested in the scenes and characters we created. I was sorry when the meeting ended, because now Bird would have to face Russell, T.T., and the rest of them.

Bird and I started walking toward the door. Russell was the first one to come over to us. T.T., Lavinia, and Mickey and Dotty followed.

"Hey, man," Russell said, "I hear you in that class where them kids tell time with a giant toy clock?" If Russell wasn't ten times my size, I would've knocked that big, simple grin off his face.

T.T. said, "They need to get a cuckoo clock, then they don't have to tell time — just listen."

"Bird is a cuckoo clock," said Russell, and they both snickered.

"Why don't you two grow up and stop making fun of people?" I yelled as we left the room. "Bird is smarter and more talented than both of you put together. He just having some trouble now, and he don't need you two mouthing off to him."

Bird walked close to me, looking ashamed. He didn't even try to defend himself. He acted as if he thought they had a right to tease him.

Before I could say anything else, Lavinia yelled as we walked down the hall, "It ain't right to make fun of them kids."

"Yeah," Dotty said, "They can't help how they are."

"You better hope nothing ever happen to you and people laugh at you, Russell and T.T.," Mickey shouted.

I was so shocked that those girls defended Bird I almost started liking them again.

"You know Russell and T.T., some things just ain't funny," Lavinia snapped.

I started feeling like Amir. He would have stood up to Russell and them without caring what anyone thought, just like I did. I guess since I was right, people just followed along with what I said.

Russell stopped walking. "We was only joking. Nobody making fun of Bird." He turned to Bird. "Man, we don't care about you being in that class. We miss you, man."

"Our class is boring when you ain't there," T.T. added.

We continued walking. "Barker shouldn't have taken you out of the class," Mickey said touching his arm. "You belong with us."

"I'm getting back in 6-3," Bird said. "Doris is going to help me."

"Right, old buddy," Russell boomed, slapping Bird on the back. "This just a little setback." Bird tried to cuff him on the side of his head, but Russell was as fast as he was big.

Russell ducked and ran down the hallway while Bird chased him and T.T., followed with his foolish "He, he, he." I know Bird was happy to be with his friends again. I was too.

I could hear the boys noisily racing down the stairs as I continued walking down the hall. Lavinia, strolling behind me, cleared her throat. "Doris, I'm surprised you're so friendly with Bird. You two having a little romance?"

I swung around and faced her nose to nose. "So what of it, Lavinia?"

She raised both of her hands and backed away. "Nothing. We just noticed you've been spending a lot of time with Yellow Bird." She glanced slyly at Mickey.

"We best friends," I said, staring right at Mickey. "And he don't start rumors like some folks around here." I glared at Lavinia.

"You joining the club?" Mickey said, looking away from me.

"Maybe," I said. "I mostly came to keep Bird company. He ain't as silly as he acts sometimes." I stared at Lavinia, knowing she'd have a smart remark to make.

Before she could open her mouth, Dotty said, "Join the club, Doris, it'll be fun."

"Well, to tell you the truth," I said, "I've already decided to."

"All right!" Dotty yelled, and she skipped down the hall in front of us as if she were jumping double Dutch. Evidently, she wasn't angry with me no more. And they were so understanding about Bird, that it caused me not to be as angry with them. It probably didn't make sense to stay mad at Lavinia because she's always been gossipy and nosey and is probably never going to change.

The boys were waiting for us when we got outside. Bird said to me, "Come on to the candy store with us, Doris."

"No, Bird," I said, clutching my notebook. "I need to study. I'll see you-all tomorrow."

"Come on, Doris," Mickey and Dotty said at the same time.

Lavinia locked her arm into mine and dragged me along. "You got to come with us, Doris, 'cause we like you again. Besides, I got some news to tell you."

Then Russell grabbed my notebook out of my hands and ran down the street, and we all chased him, laughing and clowning, until we got to the candy store. It was good to be back with my old friends again. Just like old times.

On Saturday, I had extra chores to do because Ma went shopping and Daddy was working. I didn't know what time I'd get to the Hive. I wished that I'd quit before, and now I was afraid of hurting Bird. One good thing, though, once Ma came home I wouldn't have to worry about her going back out again. Actually I really didn't have to worry about anything since I had Bird as lookout. But I was worried.

It was two o'clock when Ma finally came back. Miss Bee was probably wondering what had happened to me.

I ran downstairs and found Bird on his front stoop waiting for me. We both shivered as we walked to the Hive.

"Doris," Bird said, "You better hurry and make this money before the weather gets real cold. I'll freeze to death out here."

"Well, maybe we don't have to go," I said, thinking I'd have an easy way out.

He pulled his blue hood almost over his face and

hugged himself. "Oh no, Doris. It's okay. I've got it all planned out. I'm gonna do this spying stuff from your hallway."

"How's that?"

"If I see one of your parents or Mrs. Nicols coming down the stairs, I'll fly to the Hive, hold up my fingers, and fly back to the hallway. After all, I'm the Bird, you know." he said, flapping his arms like wings. "So, you see, Doris, you can keep your job until you get the fifty dollars."

*Great,* I thought.

He put one hand on my shoulder as we stood in front of the Hive. "Now remember, Doris. One for Ma, two for Pa, and three for Nicols."

"And four, all clear," I finished. Sometimes it's hard to have such a good best friend.

The first thing I saw was the big cloud of smoke coming out of Miss Bee's booth, which meant the Hive was busy. She looked over her divider.

"Hi, Honey Bunch, thought you weren't coming to-day," she said.

"Had to help my mother," I said, hanging up my coat.

Several customers waited their turn, and Carol and the other hairdresser worked in their booths. I cleaned towels and took appointments. Each time I answered the telephone, I tried to deepen my voice, in case my mother called again. It was awful pretending not to be here.

After I'd been there about an hour, I happened to

look toward the window and saw Bird holding up four fingers. Miss Bee saw him also.

"That your little boyfriend?"

Somebody yelled from the back, "That child too young for boyfriends!"

"He's my best friend," I said.

When I finished cleaning the towels, the same little girl whose hair I'd cornrowed before, came in with her mother. The mother said, "I was hoping you'd be here. Could you braid her hair for me?"

Needless to say, I felt proud. "Them braids don't look too bad on little girls," Miss Bee mumbled.

I braided her hair in the back of the shop in case Mrs. Nicols walked by. I still had a view of the door and the window. When I finished, I took her to her mother, who sat in the front talking to Miss Bee.

Her mother said, "That's even prettier than before." I grinned as I stood back and admired my handiwork. Not bad, I thought proudly. Not bad.

The woman gave me $3.00 and before I could finish saying thank-you, I looked up in horror to find Bird at the window holding up three fingers. I scooted to the back of the shop and nearly bumped into Carol who was washing her customer's hair. Mrs. Nicols, with her big false-tooth smile and bobbing flower hat, came tipping in through the door. Everybody in the place knew her.

"Hi, Mrs. Nicols," Miss Bee said "Haven't seen you in here since the summer of '75."

Mrs. Nicols said, "Darling, I don't have to buy good looks. I have nature's gifts."

"Sometimes even Mother Nature needs a little help, Mrs. Nicols," Miss Bee said. The customers laughed, and I didn't know what to do.

The other sink for washing hair was empty with a chair in front of it. I pushed the chair right up to the sink, laid my head back on the edge of the sink as if I was having my hair washed, and put a towel over my face.

"Girl, what is wrong with you?" Carol asked.

"I don't want that woman to see me."

"Who? Mrs. Nicols?"

"Sh-sh-sh. Yes," I whispered from underneath the towel.

Carol chuckled. "I won't say nothing."

I prayed Miss Bee didn't walk back there looking for some supplies or something and see me laying down with a towel on my face. Suddenly the telephone rang. I didn't move. Miss Bee yelled from her booth, "Honey Bunch, answer that." Thank goodness she didn't call me Doris.

I just stayed there and listened to Carol turn off the water.

"Girl, get the phone."

"I can't, Carol." My voice came out muffled.

"Where's that gal?" Miss Bee yelled again, "Somebody answer that."

Carol finally picked up the telephone — which was for her, anyway.

"Well, Mrs. Nicols, what can we do for you? Hope you ain't looking for miracles."

"I have a big affair to attend tomorrow. Can I get my hair done sometime this afternoon?"

"You have to make an appointment in advance."

I could've cried. Please don't ask me to make an appointment I said to myself.

"I'll do you a favor this once; next time you make an appointment in advance."

How am I getting out of here without Mrs. Nicols seeing me? Why did Miss Bee have to be so nice?

"Come back here in an hour."

"Thank you, darling," Mrs. Nicols said.

When Mrs. Nicols left, I removed the towel, and Carol laughed at me. "Girl, you're sweating." I told her and Miss Bee that I had to go home, but that they shouldn't tell Mrs. Nicols that I worked there on Saturdays, because she'd mention it to my mother.

I left before Mrs. Nicols came back. With the $3.00 Miss Bee gave me, I made $6.00. Now I had $21.00 and was almost halfway to Amir. But this was a close call. I couldn't go back there again, or I'd be caught for sure. I was just going to have to find another way to make the money.

I looked carefully before I stepped outside. Bird was there grinning and holding up two fingers and I saw my father at the other end of the block, coming from the subway, but he couldn't see me.

"Bird," I said as we walked down 163rd Street. "I don't think I'm going back to the Hive anymore." I told him about how I'd hid from Nicols. He laughed and put three fingers in my face. I squeezed them, and he jerked his hand away from me.

"You've got to, Doris. You just have a little more to go to see Amir."

"It just ain't right, Bird," I said. "I just can't do it anymore. But thanks for helping."

"Glad to be of some assistance," he said bowing politely. "But I still think you could make the rest."

"I will," I told Bird. "But it ain't gonna be like this."

On Monday morning, it was so cold outside that Bird wasn't even waiting for me on my stoop. As I took the shortcut through the playground, I noticed turkey and pumpkin decorations on the school windows. It was almost Thanksgiving, and I wondered how Amir was getting along.

When I passed the swings, I heard someone calling me and turned around. The twins were waving and running to catch up with me. I waited and the three of us walked to school together.

Dotty wore a plaid tam with a big green pom-pom on top. "I hear you coming to the club this afternoon, Doris."

"Yeah," I said, "but I ain't getting on no stage and acting."

Mickey adjusted her bright red tam. "Doris, I'm glad you joining. Even if you don't be in the play."

When we got to school, instead of going to the library to wait for the morning bell, I went with Mickey and Dotty to the cafeteria. Bird was there and walked over to us when we came in. He sat next to me on one of the benches, and then T.T. and Lavinia and Russell came and sat down and we all talked and joked together while we waited to line up for class.

That afternoon, Mickey and Dotty and I went to Drama Club. Dotty said more people showed up than at the first meeting last week. I think if the whole school wanted to be in the play, Mr. Washington would've let them. There were students from every grade, including Bird's class.

"Everyone quiet now." Mr. Washington stood on the stage. "The title of the play is *The Man Who Hated Christmas*. It's going to be a musical about a person who refuses to lend a helping hand. In the end though, he learns some important lessons about caring and sharing."

Mr. Washington paced back and forth staring at the floor while he talked to us. "We'll have a chorus composed of two or three students from each grade, so we'll be needing good singers and dancers."

He assigned roles next. Bird waved his hand each time Mr. Washington announced a part, but Mr. Washington ignored him. He pointed to Russell, "Would you like to play the man?"

"Yeah," Russell said, grinning. It was one of the main parts in the play. Mickey would play the part of the man's wife and Lavinia, his niece. I was relieved whenever someone else volunteered or was picked for the cast, even though Mr. Washington had told me I didn't have to act.

Bird raised his hands for part after part, but Mr. Washington pretended not to see him. I hoped he wasn't going to leave Bird out.

There were only two roles left: a shy, young boy named Joe and a homeless old woman.

Dotty waved her hands. "Can I be the old lady?" She got up and moved around like an ancient woman. Mickey jerked her back in her seat.

Mr. Washington turned to Bird. "James, I want you to play the role of Joe. Okay?"

Bird looked like he wanted to go into one of his spins. But he controlled himself and just nodded. Me, Mickey and Dotty, Lavinia, T.T., and Russell clapped and cheered. Joe was the biggest role in the play!

T.T. decided he'd rather take care of the props and make scenery. A teacher and a group of her students would operate the lights. As I was deciding what I wanted to do, Mr. Washington motioned for me to come to the stage.

"Doris, I want you to write a poem for the play."

"Mr. Washington I can't write a . . ."

He held his hand up. "James and some of the girls here have told me what a good poet you are." My face burned, and I started to get mad all over again about the poem. But then I remembered that Amir liked it. Maybe it wasn't so bad after all.

He started putting papers in his briefcase. "Anyhow, Doris, that won't be right away. For now, I need you to coach James."

"Oh yeah, I can do that, Mr. Washington."

"I knew I could depend on you." He put on his jacket. "Okay, folks. That's all until tomorrow."

Rehearsals began the following day, after school. When I got to the auditorium, Bird wasn't there yet. He could change like the weather sometimes. I hoped he'd show up.

Mr. Washington gave everyone copies of the script. "I know you'll study these so that you can memorize your parts. I expect that when we come back after the Thanksgiving weekend, all of you will know your lines perfectly." Mr. Washington smiled. Everybody moaned.

I watched the door and prayed Bird would come. Mr. Washington called some people up to the stage. Lavinia pranced around as soon as her foot hit the steps.

I turned around again to look for Bird, and just then he walked in. His blue hood was pulled way over his head. He sank down in the last row of the auditorium.

Mr. Washington called me and gave me two copies of the script. Before I had a chance to ask him how to help Bird, someone else got his attention.

I walked to the back of the auditorium and sat next to Bird. "What's wrong with you now?" I said.

"Nothing."

"Why you look so miserable? I thought you was happy about the play."

"It's the reading. Sometimes I forget words. Suppose I get on the stage and forget everything?"

"Bird, you say you want to act. You know actors have to read."

He seemed to shrink down into his hood. "Guess I was thinking about how much fun it looked to be on a stage singing and dancing."

I handed him a script. "You got stage fright and we ain't even started yet."

"You scared too, Doris."

"I know I'm scared to be in front of an audience, but I don't want to be no actress."

I read his lines to him, and he followed along with me and repeated them, sounding like someone just learning how to speak English. Barker will never let him back in the class if he sounds like this the night of the play, I thought.

We worked so hard on the play for the rest of the week, I didn't have time to think about anything else. Bird really tried, but still had a lot of trouble reading the script.

"This is different from that improvisation stuff Mr. Washington showed us," he kept saying. When Bird didn't have to read off the script and could act out the little bit he'd memorized, he was okay. But still I wondered if Bird was going to make it.

When Saturday rolled around again, I was worried about going back inside the Hive since I came so close to getting caught. I had to talk to Miss Bee, though. Daddy was at work, and Ma had to go out for most of the day. I had to mind Gerald as I anxiously waited for her to come home.

As soon as Ma got home, I went straight to Miss Bee. There was no cloud of smoke over her booth, and she sat in her chair reading the paper. I was glad she wasn't busy so that I could talk to her.

"Hi, Honey Bunch," she said when I walked in. "Where have you been today? We was real busy. We missed you."

"Hello, Miss Bee, can I talk to you about a problem I have?"

"Sure, sit down."

I took off my coat, pulled a chair up to her booth, and sat down to explain that the real reason I didn't want my mother to know I was working there was because my parents didn't want me to work.

"Well, Honey Bunch, you know I can't let you come here if your parents don't want you to."

"I know," I said sadly.

"I sure wish there was something I could do to change their minds," she said.

"I do too," I said. "But they pretty much made up their minds."

She looked at herself in the mirror and patted her hair.

"I sure will miss you, Honey Bunch, cause you're a nice girl and a good worker. By the way, don't you go to that elementary school on Cauldwell Avenue?"

"Yes," I answered.

"My nephew goes there too. He's in a play. Do you know anything about it?"

"Yeah," I said, "I'm part of it."

She opened her eyes and smiled. "Well then, I'll see you the night of the play. I'm going too."

"Miss Bee, that's wonderful. I'll see you there. And my parents will be there also." I stood up and put on my coat. "Who's your nephew?" I asked.

"You know a boy named T.T.?"

I nearly cracked up. T.T. is Miss Bee's nephew?

"He's my sister's kid. He's so excited about that play he wants the whole family to come." I wondered whether T.T. told them that he wasn't acting in it.

"Miss Bee, I'll see you the night of the play."

"Okay, Honey Bunch. And maybe I'll say hello to your parents," she said, winking.

It was beginning to snow again as I walked up 163rd Street. And even though I was out of work, I felt a thousand times better now that I'd finally quit that job and I didn't have to sneak around and lie anymore.

When I got home, Ma was in the kitchen. The apartment felt warm and cozy after the cold outside. I made hot chocolate and gave Gerald some milk while Ma fixed dinner. "Ma," I said, "I officially joined the Drama Club."

Ma beamed. "That's wonderful, Doris. I used to love to be in plays when I was in school. I'm glad you're taking part in a special activity instead of moping around here."

"I'm not going to be in it. I am just writing some and helping Bird," I said proudly.

I sat down at the table across from her and we talked about the play. She told me that she'd noticed a big change in me, but I wasn't sure what she meant. When I went back to my room to begin my homework, I realized something. For the past few weeks, I'd been thinking about a lot more things than just how I was going to visit Amir. Since I started helping Bird, I felt good. Like I used to feel when Amir was still here.

I took out Amir's letter and reread it. It didn't make me sad anymore. It wasn't that he didn't want to see me, or that he didn't need me. I knew it was time for me to answer him, because there was a lot to tell him. Maybe I couldn't visit him right away to cheer him up in person. But I knew what I had to tell Amir was going to make him happy right now.

November 16th

My Dear Amir,

How are you? Fine, I hope. I'm glad that everything is going well and that you have a nice family to be with. It's wonderful that you're with one of your brothers, at last. I read your letter to Bird, and he's glad too. It makes us happy to know that you're not lonely and you're someplace where people are treating you right. All the kids on 163rd Street still miss you too. They were all sad too when you left, but they wasn't mad because they knew it wasn't your fault that you had to leave like that.

Everything is real fine here. Dunbar Elementary is putting on a spectacular Christmas show. Everybody's part of it. Bird, the twins, Lavinia, Russell, and even T.T. I'm going to be doing writing and coaching Bird. It's real exciting, Amir.

Bird is trying very hard to do well in school and I

help him. He got in some trouble and had to be put in a special class, but if he does good in this play, I know the teacher will take him back in our class. I am going to make sure he performs so well, that she'll be on her knees, begging to take him back. I feel happy like you still here when I coach Bird. You was right about him, Amir. He's beginning to change and so am I.

You will tell me when it's okay to come and visit. It's okay if it takes you a while to get used to your new home. Anyway, I'll have to figure out another way to make money, now that Ma made me quit my job at the Hive. Meanwhile we all think about you and hope you're okay.

> Love,
> Your friend to the end,
> Doris

Ma let me walk out into the snow to mail my letter. The big snowflakes looked magical, swirling out of the sky.

Wednesday was the last rehearsal of the play before the Thanksgiving weekend. Russell and the rest of the cast had already been on stage for a few days, reading from their scripts. Since Bird had so much trouble reading, Mr. Washington wanted him to practice with me before he came on the stage.

Now Mr. Washington called Bird to the stage. "Come on up here," he said.

I stayed in my seat in the front of the auditorium.

Bird walked slowly to the stage — like he dreaded going up there.

"I wish it would snow. I wi-wish some-some . . ."

I covered my face. This was the part he'd memorized. Mr. Washington probably thought I hadn't helped Bird at all. Bird tried again. "I wish it would snow. I wi-wi . . ."

Mr. Washington jumped on the stage. He touched Bird on the shoulder. "Calm down. I know you and Doris have been practicing, right?"

I stumbled out of my seat before Bird had a chance to answer. "Mr. Washington," I said, "Bird knows that part. He said it all from memory yesterday."

Mr. Washington looked worried — almost like he felt sorry for Bird.

Bird finally found his voice. "Mr. Washington, maybe I can't do it. Maybe I should —"

"You can do this very well. I know you can, Bird." Mr. Washington didn't call him James anymore.

"When he ain't nervous, he does it good," I yelled up to the stage. I noticed that some of the other people in the cast mumbled impatiently waiting for Bird to get himself together.

"Doris, you come up too." He turned to Bird again. "Don't look at the words. Say what you remember. Ad lib, improvise the rest if you need to. Doris will help you with the words for the third scene." Mr. Washington looked around. "Where's Marcia?" She was the girl who played Bird's mother.

"She's absent today," Lavinia said.

Mr. Washington looked at me. "Doris, get on the stage with Bird and play her part."

I climbed up on the stage. I knew the part from memory because Bird and I practiced it so many times.

"I wish," Bird began. "I wish snow." He shook his head, and started again. "I wish it would snow. I wish something would . . . would . . ."

"Would happen to show me that this is a season of happiness and love," I whispered.

He repeated after me. Then I said, "Boy, you better stop wishing for snow. We have enough problems."

Bird stood up. "Isn't that supposed to happen this time of year? And isn't this supposed . . . supposed — I mean, supposed to be a season of love?" He blurted out quickly before he forgot.

I put my arm around Bird. "Son, snow and love don't go together. I hate snow." I pointed to what would be a drawing of a cracked windowpane when T.T. and his group finished the scenery.

"If it snows, do you know where it will fall?" I said.

"In this, in this —"

"Apartment," I finished for him.

"Apartment," he said, lowering his head.

"That's right son. Right through that cracked windowpane."

Bird was a little better in the next scene, replacing words he forgot with other words that made sense. I stayed at Bird's shoulder, telling him almost every word for the third scene. He was a mess, but so was everyone else, except Lavinia. I began to wonder whether

Bird being in the play was such a good idea after all. He'd never get out of the special class if he was judged by his performance now.

However, Bird relaxed when he sang his first song, "Why Is He So Mean?" His voice only squeaked once and he didn't seem at all like Yellow Bird anymore, but like shy, quiet Joe. When he finished, Lavinia said, "Bird sang his heart out."

Bird and I practiced over the Thanksgiving weekend. He was still having problems, but memorized a few more lines; however, time was moving faster than Bird was learning his lines.

Mr. Washington was trying to get us into a serious mood again when we came back to school after Thanksgiving.

"Everyone quiet," he shouted as we ran into the auditorium for rehearsal. "I have some important news."

One boy wasn't listening. He dashed to the stage. Mr. Washington practically dragged him off. "I said, 'Sit down'!"

Lavinia nudged me. "The man is beginning to act like the teachers here."

"He's beginning to look tired like them too," I said.

Mr. Washington banged a ruler on the stage. "Now people, we only have a few weeks before show time. You gotta get yourselves together." He leaned against the stage. A blotch of white paint stained his jeans. "I've invited the press to come and see you the night of the play. We might get some coverage on TV and in some local papers."

Everyone talked at once. He held up his hands. Then he jumped up onto the stage. "I told them that there was a lot of talent here at Dunbar Elementary. Now you folks aren't going to make me look like a liar, are you?"

"No!" we yelled.

"We'll give them a show they'll never forget," T.T. shouted. He wasn't even in it.

Mr. Washington started walking off the stage. "We have a lot of work to do, folks. Take your places. Mickey, Marcia, and Lavinia, stage left. Dotty, Russell, stage right."

Dotty started walking to her left. Mr. Washington shouted, "Dotty, pay attention. I said, 'Stage right'!"

She bent over and hobbled to the right like an old woman.

Everyone was messing up, and people's nerves was getting frazzled. But Mr. Washington didn't give up on us.

The next day we ate lunch in the auditorium so we could continue preparing for the play. I worked on the poem and made up two lines:

*We have two gifts for you tonight*
*Not the store-bought kind*

Mr. Washington looked over my shoulder. "That's sounding good. Say something about joy and laughter — our gifts to the audience," he said. "Bird is going to do a fine job in this play."

I put my pen down. "Do you think he could get back in our class?"

"I'm going to speak to your teacher. You've really

helped him a lot. You gave him a lot of confidence, Doris. He thinks the sun rises and sets on you."

"Bird just silly sometimes," I said looking down on my paper.

Mr. Washington walked up to the stage to help T.T. hang a large wreath as I wrote the last line of my poem.

When we went back to rehearsal after school, Mr. Washington told me he liked the poem I wrote. "Do you think you can teach it to those little ones?" He pointed to a group of kindergartners.

"What about Bird?"

"I think he can hold his own now." He brought the kids over to me. "They're all yours, Doris."

"Mr. Washington, how do I . . . ?"

A big crash interrupted me. A cardboard prop building fell on T.T.'s head, but he wasn't hurt. Mr. Washington ran to the stage, and the kids looked up at me like I was their teacher.

"Hi," I said.

One tiny boy with a very serious face said, "Is the play tomorrow?"

"No," I laughed.

"When is it?"

"A few weeks."

"Is that a long time?"

I heard Russell still missing lines. "No. Not long enough."

A girl with two dancing braids took my hand. "Am I gonna be in it too?"

"And me?" Another girl asked.

"And me too?" a boy yelled.

"Okay, okay. Calm down. Now, I want everyone to repeat after me. 'We have two gifts for you tonight.' "

They yelled, "We have two gifts for you tonight!" Then a boy with his thumb in his mouth finished after everyone else. "For you tonight," he said.

"Not the store-bought kind," I spoke very slowly.

"Not the store-bought kind!" they shouted.

"Bought kind," the same boy trailed behind.

This wasn't working. I had to think of something else. "Hey, I got it." I pointed to the girl with the braids and the serious boy.

I kneeled down and placed my hands on the boy's shoulders. "You recite the first line." I turned to the girl. "And you recite the second."

Each kid would recite one line of the poem, and everyone would recite the last two lines. I wrote out a line for each of them so they could practice it with someone at home. The girl with the dancing braids said, "This is homework?"

"Yes. Very important homework."

Those children wore me out. It was like having ten Geralds.

Bird and I practiced the play again that evening at my house, but he was still forgetting lines and not even reading the words he already knew.

"What's wrong with you?"

"I can't help it, Doris. I don't think I can be in the play," he said.

"What?"

"I can't do it. I know I can't." He balled his fist so hard his knuckles looked white.

"How can you back out now?"

"Anyone can do it. You could do my part." He loosened his fist, and his hand shook as he picked up the script. "I can't, Doris. I'll ruin the whole thing."

"You'll ruin it if you back out."

"Suppose I forget my lines and look stupid in front of all those people?"

"You'll look more stupid if you don't do it. You have a chance to go back to our class, maybe."

"I'm dumb."

"Bird, if you was dumb, you wouldn't be my best friend."

He was speechless for a minute. "I'm your best friend? You're my best friend, but I didn't know I was yours too." He stared straight ahead. "You sure you don't think I'll mess up?"

"If you forget a line, I'll be behind the curtain or in one of the crowd scenes, and I can tell you."

"I been good in that class. I thought by now I could come back to 6-3. Even the teachers keep saying how surprised they are that I know all the work in that special class."

"Bird, Mr. Washington is going to talk to Barker. When we come back to school after the holidays, I know you'll be back in our class."

"Okay, Doris. I won't back out now, that would be a dirty thing to do."

Rehearsal was a little calmer the next day. Bird re-

membered more of his lines and what he didn't remember he made up. My kindergarten kids knew the
poem perfectly. They were better than the older kids.

The stage was looking like the inside of a tenement
building. T.T. was a pretty good artist. He'd made
most of the scenery, and Lavinia — we were sure she
was going straight from Dunbar Elementary School to
Hollywood.

The school began to feel like a party was coming.
Even Barker smiled a few times. Every classroom was
decorated with paper pine trees and tinsel.

This was a happy time for all of us, because the sil-
liest things seemed special. Like the dusty, plastic
wreath with one sprig of holly that the super hung on
the building entrance every year. Ma always threat-
ened to burn that wreath, but I liked it because it was
a sign that Christmas was coming.

When I got home from rehearsal one afternoon, Ma
handed me an envelope. "You have an early Christmas
present," she said. "From your buddy upstate."

I was surprised and happy to hear from Amir.

December 15th

Dear Doris,

I was glad to get your letter. I hope you are still
fine. A lot of things been happening to me and
that's why I took so long to answer your letter. I'll be
living with the Smiths. They are adopting my
brother and I'll live with them as a foster son.

You know I told you I never wanted to live with

another family again. The Smiths are different though, from all the families I been with. They treat me like a real member of the family — a son. Mr. Smith said I should call him Dad and his wife Mom when I felt comfortable enough. I can't say it yet. Guess it's been so long since I had anyone to call Dad and Mom. But my brother calls them that; well, he's officially their son. I guess in a while I'll be able to say it too.

Mr. Smith promised that he's going to help me locate my other sisters and brothers. And one day he's going to bring me to the Bronx to visit my other family — you and Bird and the rest of the 163rd Street gang. I call you-all my other family. And if any of you want to come up here to visit later on, they said there is plenty of room.

I wish I could come down there for the play. I know it's going to be something else with Bird and Russell and all of them in it. Tell me all about it when you write again.

I'm real glad you helped Bird. I knew you could do it. He's one of the best people I know. You are too, Doris. Tell him and everyone else I said hello.

You and your family have a Merry Christmas and a Happy New Year. I still miss you, Doris. And I'm glad you keep writing to me. Write again soon.

Love,
Amir

He also made a beautiful Christmas card of a winter scene — A pretty Black girl, hanging a wreath in front of a building that looked like my building on a block that looked like 163rd Street.

I ran into the kitchen. "Ma, look at this beautiful card Amir made."

She was sitting at the kitchen table, reading the paper. "My goodness Doris, if you grin any wider your face will crack."

"Oh, Ma," I leaned on her shoulder and put the card on the table.

"That is beautiful. I think that girl looks a little like you."

She looked at the paper again, and handed me the card. "I hope you're not going to get moody on us again."

"What you mean, Ma? Me and Amir always be friends even if he ain't here."

She closed the paper. "Well, you finally got yourself together. Y'all ready for that play?"

I laughed. "I better be. Mr. Washington said, 'Ready or not, the play opens tomorrow.' "

# DUNBAR
# ELEMENTARY
# PRESENTS

DUNBAR
ELEMENTARY
PRESENTS

A half hour before show time I thought we'd never get it together. T.T. dragged out the wrong props for the first act. One of the younger kids was upset because he wondered what he'd do if he had to go to the bathroom in the middle of his speech. Russell told him, "Do it on the stage, man. The show must go on."

When Russell bent over and his pants ripped in the back, I repeated, "Don't worry, the show must go on." He started to frown, but then he laughed.

Mickey and Lavinia tried to act cool, like they was professional actresses. But Dotty and another girl bumped into each other and knocked down a picture.

And what was really making me nervous was that Bird wasn't here yet. Mr. Washington, looking as old and tired as the teachers at Dunbar, came over to me for the fifth time. "He isn't here yet? Where is he?"

"I don't know, Mr. Washington." I wouldn't tell him that Bird had been talking about leaving the play. I didn't want Mr. Washington to have a heart attack. I couldn't believe that Bird wouldn't show.

I walked over to T.T. who was hanging the picture of the cracked window. "Did Bird say anything to you about not showing up?"

He straightened out the picture. "Hey Miss Doris, you sure look fine, sweetness."

"Oh shut up, T.T. Did you hear from Bird?"

"No. He'll be here, unless he got sick or something." He took my hand and turned me around. "My, but I love your wine-colored dress and the beautiful beads in your hair. Are they real ivory?"

I pulled away from him. "T.T., you act too foolish."

He lifted my hand like he was going to kiss it, but he kissed his own instead. "Oh, and are those new shoes you're wearing?"

"T.T., you better go back to your scenery." I jerked my hand away from his. Suddenly Mr. Washington leaped up on the stage.

"Doris, we have an emergency." He looked desperate. I knew it was something about Bird.

"We're in a serious jam. Marcia is sick, and she can't make the show."

I was relieved it wasn't Bird. "What you want me to do, Mr. Washington?"

"You gotta play her part. You're the only one who can do it."

I felt faint. My hands trembled and everything in front of me looked like a blur. "No, Mr. Washington. I can't. I'll make a fool of myself."

"Doris," he said, squeezing my hand, "you're the same size she is so you can fit into that long skirt and shawl and you read that part perfectly at rehearsal."

I shook my head and tried to swallow. "I can't do it. I'll forget everything soon as I see the audience."

At that moment, Bird walked over to us. Was I ever glad to see him! Mr. Washington grabbed him by the arm. "About time you got here," he said. "Doris has to play the part of your mother. Make her get dressed and ready to go onstage." He stomped away angrily.

I was almost in tears. Bird looked happy. "What took you so long to get here?"

Bird made a funny little dance step, moving his feet back and forth quickly.

"My mother called to wish me luck. And she's coming home after the holidays."

"Bird, I can't do it. You and me onstage together? It'll be a disaster."

He patted my shoulder. "I'll help you."

"I'm supposed to be helping you," I said.

He put his arm around my shoulder. "We just mess up together, Yellow Bird and Doris. You know what?" He grinned. "My father might come too."

I walked backstage. "That's nice, Bird. Your father can watch me and you look stupid together." I forgot all about my nice words of encouragement to Bird.

"Come on, Doris," Bird said. "We can do it. We'll be great!"

I changed to that old long gray skirt and covered my nice hairdo with the shawl, and shook while I dressed.

Mickey said, "You'll be okay, Doris." Then she stifled a big laugh. We didn't get ourselves together until seven o'clock and the show was supposed to start at six thirty. The audience was restless. I peeped from behind the curtain and saw my mother and father sitting in the front row with Gerald. Mickey and Dotty's mother squeezed herself down one of the side aisles.

There was a commotion in the middle row, where the Nit Nowns, those five sisters from Union Avenue sat looking like five Christmas trees. They wore red sequined hats and green coats and enough bangles and beads to open up a five and ten cent store. I didn't see Miss Bee yet and hoped she'd show up.

Mrs. Nicols didn't have chick nor child in Dunbar Elementary, but she sat there with her little flowered hat in December like she was at a Broadway opening.

A tall man walked slowly down the middle aisle. It was Bird's father, and as usual he didn't crack a smile.

The lights dimmed, and the audience was quiet. My heart raced like a jet. I'd die before the second scene. The curtain parted and the six kindergarten students came to the middle of the stage.

*We have two gifts for you tonight,*
*Not the store-bought kind.*

*Our gifts are joy and laughter bright,*
*Which can be hard to find.*

*Once you have received them*
*You will understand,*

*That gifts like these are placed within*
*Our hearts and not our hands.*

*So open up your hearts real wide*
*Accept our special offer.*

*Each of us will step inside*
*And give you joy and laughter.*

They were perfect. The audience gave them a big hand, and they ran off the stage jumbled up together and all smiles.

Then the spotlight fell on Bird, who sat cross-legged in the center of the stage. "I wi-wish . . ." His hands shook a little and his voice quivered. I crossed my fingers. Please don't let him forget his lines. It was bad enough I had to come out there a nervous mess.

He started again, breathing deeply, like Mr. Washington had told us to do.

"I wish it would snow. I wish something would happen to show me that this is a season of happiness and love," he said in a loud clear voice. All his nervousness was gone.

Bird looked stage left in my direction. Lavinia said, "Go on Doris, that's your cue."

It felt like my feet had grown big rusty roots. Lavinia gave me a push, and I stumbled on stage. I opened my mouth but nothing came out. Then I heard Gerald yell "Doris!" I was too humiliated.

Bird stood up like he was supposed to. He repeated his last line and walked over to me. "I wish it would snow!" he shouted in my ear. Then he whispered out the side of his mouth. "Say, 'Boy, you better stop wishing for snow.' "

I grabbed Bird's neck — anything to hold on to.

"Boy, you better stop wishing for snow," I mumbled.

Somebody in the back of the auditorium yelled, "We can't hear you." It sounded like one of the Nit Nowns.

Bird said, "Mother, why you so upset?" That wasn't one of his lines. He turned his back to the audience. "Look in my face, Doris and make believe this is rehearsal," he whispered.

I stared at Bird like I was in a daze. "We have enough problems," I shouted. "You better stop wishing for snow."

He put his hand on my arm and smiled, and I only looked at him.

"We have enough problems," I repeated.

Bird held my shaking hand. "Isn't it supposed to snow this time of year? Isn't this supposed to be a season of love?" Bird was perfect.

"Snow and love don't go together," I yelled stiffly.

"Son," Bird whispered.

"Son!" I shouted. "I hate snow."

I forgot to point to the window. Bird pointed and said my line for me. "If it snows, it will fall in this apartment. Through that crack in the window."

"Yes, son. It sure will." We were ad-libbing now. I stared in Bird's face.

There were three knocks. That was my cue. "Who is it?" I tried to say with feeling.

"It's me! Mr. Rancid's niece." That was Lavinia. She was stage right. I saw her whip off the scarf she'd been wearing just before she made her entrance on stage. If there was an academy award for students in elementary school plays, Lavinia would've won it. Her hair was cornrowed in a beautiful circular design with tiny red beads. Some people clapped as soon as she walked on. Guess it was her family.

Lavinia put one hand on her hip and the other in my face. "I come for the rent."

"The rent's not due until tomorrow," I said, still looking at Bird, even though I was supposed to be talking to Lavinia.

"Tomorrow is Christmas. Nobody's collecting rents tomorrow," Lavinia replied.

All I had to do now was cry. I cried for real, because I felt like crying anyway. "We don't have the money right now."

Lavinia spread her arms. "How can you expect to live in a wonderful place like this for free?"

"Wonderful place?" Bird leaned in her face. "You call this a wonderful place?"

"It has a roof, doesn't it? Look, kid, you know my uncle's motto — if you don't pay, then you can't stay in this building."

The way she said it, the audience laughed and clapped. She didn't have a nervous bone in her body.

Bird pointed to the ceiling. "The roof is falling." He put his arm around me. I still boo-hooed. "And my poor old mother is ill."

"My uncle says I have to get the money today." Lavinia stamped her foot and crossed her arms.

"Have a heart, miss," Bird said. "Look at my dear old Mom."

I cried louder. I couldn't wait for the scene to end.

"You are ungrateful. You want to live in a lovely place like this for free."

Bird stepped out to the middle of the stage for the first song. The music teacher played a chord. I hoped Bird's voice wouldn't go into a squeak.

> *Mean to us*
> *Why is he so mean to us?*
> *It must be great fun to be*
> *mean to us.*

> *He lets the roof fall on our heads.*
> *He won't give us any heat,*
> *and if we're late with the rent,*
> *he'll throw us in the street.*

Somebody in the audience yelled, "Sing it!"
Bird spread his legs and arms:

> *Mean to us*
> *Why is he so mean to us?*

Now Lavinia sang her song. She stepped in front of Bird and pointed her finger in his face.

> *Ungrateful, that's what you are.*
> *Ungrateful and a bore.*
> *Always demanding*
> *Never understanding that*
> *My uncle is a shining star.*

Then they sang together:

> *Mean to us*
> *Why is he so mean to us?*

*Ungrateful, that's what you are.*
*Ungrateful and a bore.*

They got a real big hand and I sneaked off the stage. Maybe since they were so good, people hadn't noticed how bad I was. Luckily, I didn't have to go on again until the second act, and I only had to say a few lines.

I was still trembling, but Mr. Washington was smiling. "Was it so bad, Doris? You really helped us out of a spot."

Bird finished his scene. He ran over to us. "How was I? Was I good?"

Mr. Washington gave him a big hug. "Man, I told you you could do it."

I kissed him on his cheek. "Bird, you was great and you saved my life too," I said.

Lavinia rushed off the stage and changed for her next scene. Dotty practiced her old-lady walk.

People laughed and clapped when the curtain opened again. Russell, wearing a burgundy velvet smoking jacket, sat with his legs crossed in a big overstuffed chair. He held a long cigar, unlit, of course.

Russell really looked like a fifty-year-old man. T.T. had taken a blackboard eraser and rubbed the white chalk dust from it on the sides of Russell's hair to make it look like he was graying.

"Ah, hum," Big Russell cleared his throat. "Anybody don't pay up their rent is losing the beautiful living quarters I provide."

Mickey was Mrs. Rancid, the man's wife. "But dear,

it's Christmas," she said. Mickey wore one of her mother's wigs and a wide flair skirt.

"So what does that have to do with anything? I ain't Santa Claus. I have bills to pay too." Russell banged his fist so hard on the table that the lamp started to fall off, but Mickey caught it.

Mr. Washington put his face in his hands.

"They don't pay — they can't stay. That's my motto," Russell's voice boomed.

I wasn't as nervous for the scene in the second act. But I still wasn't no actress. All I had to say was, "My son, you're like a shining light on a cold, dark night." I got the words out, but my voice cracked a little.

Lavinia, Mickey, and two other girls did a dance for the party scene. One of the girls accidentally tripped up Mickey, and Mickey's wig fell off. Lavinia did a spin reached down and slapped the wig, lopsided, back on Mickey's head.

The audience thought it was part of the dance; they loved it.

Then Bird, Lavinia, and the twins sang their number together.

> *He has changed*
> *Are you listening?*
> *He's not strange*
> *this Christmas.*
>
> *He's a beautiful sight*
> *He's happy and bright*
> *The mean old man has changed.*

The audience clapped along while they sang.

Then the whole cast slowly walked on the stage singing.

> *He's given us a new roof.*
> *He's gonna plaster all the holes.*
> *He's painting everybody's apartment*
> *and promises never to let us get cold.*
>
> *He has changed and we love him.*
> *No complaints about him*
> *It's a wonderful sight*
> *We're happy tonight*
> *The mean old man has changed.*

Dotty, Bird, Lavinia, and Russell did their dance routine. The audience clapped them on. Dotty kicked her leg so high her left shoe flew off her foot. The audience cheered. I almost cried I laughed so hard.

When the number ended, the audience went wild. Cameras flashed, and a reporter from a local paper talked to Mr. Washington. Who would think that you could have singing, dancing, and acting like that at our school, in the Bronx?

The whole company, as Mr. Washington called us, took part in the finale. The first graders had their little candlelighting ceremony. Then we all sang "Joy to the World" and the audience joined in with us. The ending was superb. Mrs. Nicols even said so later.

The audience clapped, cheered, yelled, and stood up. Bird and Lavinia got the biggest hands of all. As long as people clapped, Bird kept bowing. Mr. Washington got up on the stage and stood next to me.

"That boy's hooked," he said. "I see it in his eyes."

Bird nearly fell when he jumped off the stage. He was trying to get to his father, but everyone crowded around him. Then came the biggest shock of all. Mrs. Barker shook his hand. "You did a wonderful job," she said. "I'm impressed."

Mrs. Nicols hugged Bird and then stepped back and held him at arms' length, the flower on her hat bobbing back and forth. "A star is truly born," she said.

Bird finally reached his father, and I saw Mr. Washington shake his father's hand and start talking to him. Mr. Towers actually smiled.

I found my mother and father talking to Mrs. Nicols. Gerald ran over to me, and I bent down and kissed him.

"Doris," he squealed.

"He got so excited when you stepped out on that stage," Ma said.

Daddy gave me a kiss and a red rose. "To my little star," he said. "And I don't care what nobody says, you were the best one up there."

I laughed, "Daddy, I was awful. I wasn't even supposed to be in it."

Ma gave me a kiss. "I'm proud of you, girl. You sure helped Bird get his act together."

I waved to the Nit Nowns, and looked for Miss Bee. T.T. had his whole family onstage showing them the scenery he made, but I didn't see her among them.

"Hi, Honey Bunch."

I turned around and there she was in her high heels

and a beige suit, with her coat draped over her arms. "Hi, Miss Bee! You look nice."

"How are you, Miss Bee?" my mother said. Daddy smiled and nodded in her direction.

Miss Bee put her arm around my shoulders. "Mr. and Mrs. Williams, you should be proud of your daughter."

"We are," my mother said quickly.

"She's a wonderful young lady," Miss Bee continued. "I've missed her since she stopped helping me out in the shop. Even brought in a customer." She stopped to clear her throat. "Braided a little girl's hair and the child's mama came back looking for her."

"Doris is a good worker, huh?" Daddy said.

"Yes," Miss Bee said squeezing my shoulders. "She's a gem. If you ever change your mind about letting her work, she's got a job waiting at the Hive. Me and the other ladies will look out for her." She winked at me, and my father shook her hand.

"We try to raise her right," he said proudly.

"Have a Merry Christmas," she called over her shoulder and tipped away on her high heels.

"That woman sure did like you," Ma said. "You made some impression on her for just having gone that *once*." She looked at me closely, and I picked up Gerald.

Daddy smiled. "Quite a character, but she seems like an okay lady."

I agreed. Miss Bee really talked up for me.

Lavinia was on the stage having her picture taken. The twins were with their mother and one of the Nit

Nowns. Bird's father still smiled and talked to Mr.
Washington. Whatever Mr. Washington was saying
must've been good, because Bird was standing next to
them, beaming like a flashlight.

My parents started talking to a lady who lives on our
block, and I walked over to Bird. With his hair brushed
back and his suit that fit right, he was kind of hand-
some.

"I told you that you'd be great in the play," I said.

His smile could've lit a dark cave. "Only 'cause you
helped me."

Suddenly, a boy holding a camera came up to us.
"You a good actor," he said to Bird. "Let me take a
picture of you for the yearbook."

"Only if you take my co-star too," he shouted pulling me next to him. We grinned while we stood there
side by side with our arms around each other's shoulders.

When he finished, the boy asked, "What's your names
again, so I can write them for the caption?"

"Just write Yellow Bird and me," I said, and we
laughed.

There was a smile everywhere I looked. This was
truly a season of love.


January 30th

My Dear Amir,

I hope you are fine and happy. The sun is shining here on 163rd Street even though it's snowing. I
hope the sun is shining where you are too.

Remember the letter I wrote you for Christmas

where I told you how wonderful the play turned out? Well it must have been better than I thought. Barker took Bird back in our class the beginning of this month. His performance must've *really* impressed her.

Mr. Washington explained to Barker what was wrong and now he gets special tutoring in reading. He's got something called dyslexia. It's real hard for him to read even though he's really smart. Barker doesn't pick on him anymore. She lets him tell her the answers to written tests and then he writes them down later. Bird does everything we do except it takes him a little longer.

Mickey says that Barker feels guilty because she treated Bird so mean. But I think she learned to see inside of Bird — remember you used to tell me about seeing the inside of things so you understand them better?

Bird is so different. You wouldn't believe it if you saw him. He's got to work hard, but he's doing it. Passing everything. T.T. told him, "You ain't no more fun." Remember they said the same thing about me? Bird still makes us laugh, but not in class. And guess what else? I made the honor roll this term. All that time I spent helping Bird helped me, too. I guess I was studying more than usual without knowing it!

Here's the best news of all. My parents finally gave me permission to work at the Hive on Saturdays — if I don't have to help Ma in the house.

It's funny, Amir. I still think about you all the time. But it's different now. It's like you're here with me, even when you're not. You helped me to see inside Bird, and now he's a real best friend. Just like you. It's like you said to me once. We're not really separated. Together we'll make things be. I know that some day we'll all live on the same block again. I just know it. Write soon.

Your friend to the end.
Love,
Doris